THAT'S WHAT FRIENDS ARE FOR

THAT'S WHAT FRIENDS ARE FOR

Carol Adorjan

AN
APPLE
PAPERBACK

SCHOLASTIC INC.
New York Toronto London Auckland Sydney

ISBN 0-590-42454-8

12 11 10 9 8 7 6 5 4 3 2 1   0 1 2 3 4 5/9

Printed in the U.S.A.   40
First Scholastic printing, April 1990

For
The Real Susie

Warm Heart, Curious Mind, Dimples and All

1

"**S**omething important's going to happen," Mary Agnes Gardner announced, as soon as Mrs. Anson had closed the door of the classroom behind her. Their sixth-grade teacher, Mrs. Anson, had not been called out of the classroom for some trivial reason. Mary was certain of that.

Tommy Brennan snorted. "Here we go again," he said, looking smugly around the classroom.

Nina Ross ignored him. "Like what, Mags?" she asked, her round face lit with interest.

"I'm not sure," Mary said, "but it's going to change things."

Nina leaned forward in her chair. "What things?" she asked.

Mary sighed. "Just . . . things, Nina. I don't know *what* things."

A murmur swept through the class. Mrs. Anson often left the classroom, leaving one of her students in charge. Usually, she came back in a few minutes with freshly photocopied stacks of some

1

paper or other. Sometimes, like today, the principal, Mr. Ballard, or some other teacher called her out of the room. At least once, she had left the room to stand against the wall outside the door. Matt Tucker had seen her. Whatever the reason, it was never *important*. This time she'd left Mary in charge.

"Where'd you get your information?" Richard Bianchi asked.

"Yeah," Tommy sneered. "How do *you* know?" The freckles on his nose seemed to run together like raindrops forming a puddle.

At the front of the room, Mary shifted from one foot to the other. She knew she should ignore the boys' challenge, but, at the same time, she felt the need to defend herself. "I . . . have a . . ." She glanced at Greg Hopkins. He shook his head slightly as if to warn her not to say another word, but it was too late. ". . . feeling," she finished.

Greg rolled his dark eyes and slid down in his chair so that all Mary could see of him was the side of his head. With the sun shining in from the window behind him, his ear looked red.

Tommy's eyes widened into two circles. "Hear that, everybody?" he said. "Mags has a *feeling*." Pretending to bite his fingernails anxiously, he added, "Oh, wow! That really scares me," in a high-pitched voice.

Everyone laughed.

A warm flush spread across Mary's face to her ears. They felt as red as Greg's looked. But she couldn't give in to her embarrassment. She had a responsibility here, feelings or no. Mrs. Anson had put her in charge of the class. "We're supposed to be doing math," she scolded and opened her workbook.

Tommy stepped to the front of the class. "Let's take a vote," he said. "Who wants to do math?"

A wave of grumbling broke over the class. No one wanted to do math.

"I've got an idea." Tommy turned toward Mary. "Why don't you just give us the answers? Save everybody some time."

Mary crossed her arms over her chest and glared at him. "That wouldn't be fair," she said. "Besides, I don't know the answers."

Tommy looked shocked. "*You* don't know the answers?"

Mary narrowed her eyes. She was one of the smartest people in the class, but to expect her to look at a three digit by three digit multiplication problem and come up with the answer was asking too much. "No one knows the answers unless they work the problems."

"Really?" Tommy's expression was serious, but Mary saw a teasing glint in his blue eyes. "I had a *feeling* you might have a *feeling* what they were."

Amy Laidlaw snickered. "Honestly, Mags, you and your *feelings*."

Mary's ears throbbed with heat. She untucked her brown hair from behind them and let it fall forward.

Greg Hopkins popped to his feet. His dark eyes sparked. "You're just jealous because you don't have *any* feelings," he accused Amy.

Mary sighed gratefully. She and Greg had been friends for a long time, since fourth grade when he and his family had moved into the new house around the corner from her own. She could always depend on him to stick by her, even when she'd set herself up for a fall as she had just done.

Amy's mouth narrowed to the size of a pencil line. "I do so have feelings! *Real* feelings about *real* things." Then she pitched her math workbook at him.

Greg ducked. The book sailed past him. Tommy raised his arm to deflect it. The manual seemed to hover in midair before changing direction. Horrified, the class watched it fly right for Mrs. Anson's African violets on the windowsill. When the book landed — Plop! — against the window, two purple flowers dropped to its soft, glossy cover.

A low whistle escaped the cage of Greg's teeth. "I have a feeling Mary was right," he said.

Everyone knew what he meant. When Mrs. Anson saw that her violets had lost their heads, something out-of-the-ordinary would certainly happen.

"Here she comes!" Matt Tucker announced.

Mary wrote some numbers on the board. Retrieving her workbook from the windowsill, Amy tucked the broken violets back into the pot. Everyone else scurried to their places, opened their math workbooks, took a deep breath, and held it.

Mrs. Anson paused outside the room. Through the window in the door, the class watched her curly head bob up and down. She was talking to someone. Someone short.

Finally, she threw open the door and waltzed in. Her long, burgundy skirt danced around her calves, and the low heels of her black pumps *clack-clack*ed on the wood floor as she paraded to the front of the room. She was smiling. Her eyes flitted around the room passing lightly over the violets. Her smile never faded.

The class let out an audible breath.

Mrs. Anson laughed. "It sounds as though you've all been working hard."

Mary opened her mouth to speak. She felt duty-bound to say that they had finished no math and that one of the violets had accidentally met with sudden, violent death.

The class cut her off with, "Yes, Mrs. Anson," said in a single loud, clear voice.

Mrs. Anson beamed. "That's fine," she said to the class. Then, "Thank you, Mary Agnes, I knew I could count on you."

Mary felt as if her ears were poking through her hair, red-hot — a sign of guilt, as if she, personally, had kept the class from doing the assigned work and had decapitated the violets with her own hand. She slunk to her place in the fourth row. Sliding her gaze toward Greg, she sank down into her seat across from his.

"I warned you," he hissed. He was referring to her psychic feelings. She knew he was right. But she had been right, too, more than once. And if she waited until *after* something happened to say she had a feeling — like last year when their class had won the division football championship — the teasing would be even worse than it had been today.

Mrs. Anson announced, "Class, I have a surprise for you." She glanced to her left. Then, she whirled to look behind her. "Suzanne?" she said,

6

a confused expression on her face. She started towards the door. There, she leaned around the corner and coaxed someone forward.

After an expectant pause, a petite blonde girl stepped into the room in — of all things — a dress! with puffed sleeves!

Surprised expressions on their faces, the class froze as Mrs. Anson put an arm around the girl's shoulder and led her to the front of the room.

"Class," the teacher said, "I'd like you to meet Suzanne Marsden." Her tone was proud, as though she were introducing someone special. Taking two steps back, her arms outstretched towards Suzanne, she added with a flourish, "Your new classmate!"

2

Suzanne Marsden stood center stage, her hands cupped demurely at her plaid-ribboned waist, her eyes downcast, dimpling her dimples. Through the holes in the green windowshades, light shone on her like spotlights.

For several seconds, everyone was absolutely still. Then, as if a dam had opened, letting water flood through, a murmur swept through the room. People squirmed in their seats trying to get a better view of the new girl. Some muttered comments. Others shot inquiring glances at Mary.

Staring right at Mary, Tommy said, "So this is it? The important event?" loud enough for everyone to hear.

Mary ignored him. Even if she'd wanted to answer, she wouldn't've known what to say. Suzanne's arrival must have been what she had predicted. What else could it be? But was the addition of a new member to the class going to be so important? She wasn't certain. She sighed. Having feelings about future happenings and knowing exactly what they meant were not always one and the same.

Mrs. Anson clapped her hands together. "Attention, class," she said. "We wouldn't want Suzanne to get the wrong impression of us, would we?" She spoke proudly, as if Suzanne were a visiting celebrity.

It's the dress, Mary thought. Mrs. Anson went way beyond the school dress code, which required neatness. She actually believed girls should wear dresses, and no one should wear jeans. *Ever.*

Everyone snapped to attention. Straightening to their full heights, the boys seemed to grow before the girls' eyes.

Suzanne didn't notice. She was looking at her shoes.

The class looked at her shoes, too. Delicate black flats. Then, the girls looked down at their own shoes, bright, colored athletic shoes with brand names written on them. There was a shuffling sound as they tucked their feet back under their chairs.

Mrs. Anson beamed down at the new girl. "We're all happy you've joined us, Suzanne," she

9

said. "Let's give Suzanne an old-fashioned welcome." She raised her arms as if she were about to conduct an orchestra. "Welcome, Suzanne. We're glad you're here," she intoned.

"Welcome, Suzanne. We're glad you're here," the class echoed.

Suzanne Marsden glanced up. She smiled slightly at the class. Her dimples deepened. "Please call me Susie," she said.

The boys hooted.

Amy grimaced and mouthed, "Susie," silently.

"Let's see . . . Susie. Where shall we put you?" Mrs. Anson said as she glanced around the room. "Amy," she directed, "please take your things and move to the empty seat next to Matthew."

Amy sat in the first seat in the third row directly in front of Greg. Narrowing her eyes, she said, "Yes, Mrs. Anson," and started slamming her books together.

Mary glanced at Greg. He grinned at her but gave no indication of his feelings about the new seating arrangement. She'd ask him about it before lunch.

While she waited for Amy to make the switch, Mrs. Anson told the class, "We'll put Susie up front until she catches on to our routine." To Susie she said, "I think you'll like it here. Merredith Heights hasn't all the . . . facilities some of the bigger schools have — "

"That's for sure," Richard muttered. Merredith Heights didn't even have lockers. The school was so old-fashioned it still had coatrooms at the back of every classroom. And regular desks with attached chairs set in precise rows.

Ignoring the disturbance, Mrs. Anson went on, " — but small schools have many advantages." Then she said, "Mary Agnes?"

Mary stood up. "Yes, Mrs. Anson?"

"How would you like to be Susie's . . . big sister for a while? Show her around. Answer any questions she might have."

Mary hesitated. She glanced at Susie. She looked nice enough, but how could Mary be sure she'd like her? And did Mrs. Anson expect her to spend all her time with the new girl? That would certainly change *her* life — at least for a while. If only she could talk it over with Greg before she accepted this new responsibility. She looked at him, but he was looking at Susie.

"I don't think you'll have any trouble adjusting, Susie," the teacher said. "Mary Agnes will help you over any rough spots."

Mary was miffed. She had thought she had a

choice here, but, apparently, she'd been wrong. It had already been decided.

"I'm sure there won't be any problem," Mrs. Anson went on. "This class is particularly outgoing and friendly."

On the way to her newly assigned place, Amy poked Mary with her elbow. "She always picks you for everything," she muttered.

Susie slipped into her chair just as the lunch bell rang. She turned toward Mary. "What now, Mary Agnes?" she asked.

Repeating "Mary Agnes!" Greg laughed.

Susie looked confused. "Did I say something wrong?"

Mary shook her head. "No one calls me *Mary Agnes* except Mrs. Anson," she said.

"Call her *Mags*," Greg said.

Susie's blue eyes widened in disbelief. "Mags? Really?"

"That's what everyone calls me," Mary said. "Greg started it. It's for my initials: Mary Agnes Gardner."

Suzanne nodded. "So what do we do now?" she asked.

"Lunch," Greg answered.

Susie smiled at him. Her teeth were straight and white. "Oh," she said simply.

Greg joined the other boys on their way to the coatroom.

Mary watched after him. She was hoping to talk to him before he got away, but she couldn't leave Susie. "We eat in the gym," Mary told her. "Well, actually, at lunchtime it's not a gym; it's a lunchroom. There're tables in the wall."

Susie looked mystified. "In the wall?"

"We don't *eat* in the wall — I didn't mean that. What I mean is, we don't have a cafeteria or anything like that," Mary explained. "We have to bring our lunch, except when we have Hot Dog Day or whatever, but we don't have those days too often, and we always know about them ahead of time. We have to sign up. But we *always* eat in the gym. Assemblies are there, too. The tables fold up and down. Out of the wall. They're *down* when we eat. When lunch is over, they go back up into the wall." She chuckled. "Not by themselves. Different kids — whoever's assigned — put them back up so — "

"Lunch period'll be over by the time you finish telling her about it, Mags," Amy interrupted.

"She always gives long explanations," Nina told Susie.

"I'm just doing what Mrs. Anson asked me to," Mary said. She got to her feet.

"Where's your lunch, Susie?" Jennifer asked.

"You can eat with us," Laurie said.

"*I'm* supposed to be her big sister," Mary objected. "She has to eat with me."

"We all eat together," Amy reminded her.

"Even so," Mary replied. "Mrs. Anson asked me to show her around, so I should be the one to take her to the gym."

"Let's let Susie decide," Jennifer suggested.

Everyone looked at Susie expectantly.

Still sitting at her desk, Susie smiled up at them. "I'm going home for lunch," she said. "My father's picking me up." She slid out from behind her desk and sailed out of the room.

Intending to escort her to the exit, Mary trailed after her. "Wait up!" she called, but Susie was already on her way through the front door.

Greg came up beside her. "What's up?" he asked.

"Nothing. I was just" — Mary shrugged — "helping Susie."

Greg looked around. "Where is she?"

"She went home for lunch."

Greg laughed. "So what're you going to do? Stand here till she gets back?" he teased.

Mary grinned at him. "And miss lunch?" she said. "No one's *that* important."

3

When Mary joined the other girls at their usual table, Amy was saying, "She must be rich."

"What makes you think so?" Nina asked.

"Her father picked her up, didn't he?" Amy explained.

"What's that prove?" Mary asked.

"If he can come pick her up in the middle of the day, then he must not work," Amy said.

"Maybe he's a boss or something," Laurie suggested. "They can get off work whenever they want."

"Then he's still rich," Amy said.

"What about the van?" Nina put in.

"What van?" Mary asked.

"The one she went home in. Didn't you see it?"

Mary shook her head. She'd been standing in the hall when Susie left.

"We watched from the window," Nina said. "It's

a rusty old wreck. Even our car's better than that."

"Everybody's car's better than that," Jennifer put in.

"Sometimes rich people are like that," Amy argued. "They ride around in old wrecks and wear strange clothes."

Laurie nodded. "Maybe that's how they get rich."

They fell silent, thinking about that.

Although Mary didn't understand why, her friends' focus on Susie made her uncomfortable. Deliberately changing the subject, she said, "I can't wait till next year when we have a real cafeteria."

Next September, the Merredith Heights sixth grade would move on to junior high, which was housed in a newer building on the other side of town. In addition to a separate cafeteria, it had two gyms, and an auditorium. Since the first day of school, the class had been focused on two things: their position as the oldest in the school and their future status. Mary was determined not to let the arrival of a new classmate change that.

"I just can't wait," she repeated.

As though on cue, Laurie said, "Me neither. Just think: we'll be able to order whatever we want!"

"Right," Mary said.

"I can't wait till we have comfortable seats for assemblies instead of these old folding chairs," Amy said.

"Right," Mary said again.

"And imagine playing volleyball and not having your shoes stick to the floor!" Jennifer said.

"Right," Mary repeated. She felt like a cheerleader urging her team to victory.

A hoot rose up from the next table, and then the boys scattered, leaving Richard sitting alone, an open milk carton on the back of each hand.

"Not again," Jennifer said.

Mary shook her head. "He keeps falling for that trick." To Richard, she said, "Why do you keep falling for that trick?"

"I thought I could do it this time," Richard mumbled. He raised one hand off the table slowly, held it in the air for several seconds, and then lowered it carefully so as not to spill the milk. Sighing heavily, he tried the other hand.

"Use your mouth," Mary said. She meant for him to remove one carton with his teeth. That would free a hand so that he could replace both cartons on the table without spilling any milk.

For several seconds, he looked confused. Then, his face brightened with understanding. "Help!" he said.

The girls exchanged *can-you-believe-it* glances.

"Richard!" Mary said as she got to her feet.

"You told me to use my mouth," Richard said.

"I didn't mean like that!"

"Wait a minute. I've got an idea," Richard said as he raised one hand again.

Mary knew what was coming. "Richard! Don't!" she warned.

Too late.

He dropped his hand suddenly. The carton teetered and tipped, splashing milk as it headed for the floor. Richard grinned sheepishly. "It didn't work," he said.

"Boys are so stupid," Amy said.

On the playground, Marisa Sanchez, who lived across the street and had gone home for lunch, was standing beside Susie. Her blue-black hair gleamed in the afternoon sun. When she saw the other girls, she took Susie's arm and marched toward them.

"She's still wearing that awful dress," Amy said.

Even Mary, who thought the fine wale corduroy dress looked nice on Susie, was surprised she hadn't changed into jeans or slacks when she saw everyone else wearing them.

Running backwards for a catch, Tommy stumbled into Marisa and Susie's path.

"Watch it," Marisa barked.

Susie flashed her dimpled smile.

"She's actually smiling at Tommy!" Laurie said.

As she approached the other girls, Susie's smile widened. Her dimples deepened. She seemed bubbly and confident. Not at all the shy girl she had appeared to be this morning.

"They are so nice," she said and tossed a glance over her shoulder at the boys.

Jennifer groaned. "Nice. Nice? Nice!" She repeated the word as if she'd just heard it for the first time and was trying to figure out its meaning.

"At my other school, the boys were awful," Susie said.

"Susie went to school in the city," Marisa announced. She said it as though it was important information that only she knew.

"Boys are awful everywhere," Laurie scoffed.

Susie smiled at the boys, who were huddled a few feet away, watching.

"Did you ever see anybody so boy crazy?" Amy whispered to Mary.

Mary nudged her disapprovingly.

Tommy did a handstand and fell over on his back. Scrambling to his feet, he said, "I meant to do that."

Susie laughed. "I thought it would be hard coming to a new school," she said. "But everybody's so nice."

"Susie's mother makes candy," Marisa announced importantly.

No one quite understood what that had to do with anything, but they welcomed the change of subject.

"What kind?" Nina asked.

"All kinds," Susie answered.

Like a broken record, Jennifer kept shaking her head and mumbling, "Nice," as she cast glances at the boys.

Laurie's eyes widened. "Chocolate creams?"

Susie nodded. "She's in the business."

"The candy-making business?" Laurie looked as though she'd just discovered a gold mine.

"Rich just like I said," Amy murmured in Mary's ear.

"Where's her store?" Laurie asked.

"She makes it at home," Susie said.

"But where does she *sell* it?" Laurie persisted.

Her friends translated that to mean, *Where can I buy it?* Candy — especially chocolate creams — was Laurie's weakness.

"She takes orders," Susie told her.

"What does your father do?" Amy asked.

"Helps my mother," Susie said.

Amy nodded smugly.

Laurie stepped back and put her hands on her hips. Her expression was disbelieving. "Your mother makes candy at home," she repeated. "It's her business."

Susie nodded again.

"Then how come you aren't" — Laurie looked her up and down — "fat?"

Mary blushed as if she'd been the one to ask that rude question.

"Because I don't like candy," Susie explained simply. Then she smiled at Mary. "I never saw anybody's ears get so red!"

Although her tone wasn't unkind, Mary felt a sting in the words. Obviously, she was as tactless as Laurie. Tactless and boy crazy. And probably not too smart. Besides her dimples, Mary wondered what else Susie had to recommend her.

4

When the bell rang, all the girls vied for a place in line beside Susie. Amy, who minutes ago had called the girl boy crazy, won out.

"Susie's mother has a candy business," Laurie told Matt as the class assembled.

"No wonder she's so . . . sweet," Matt said, looking around at everyone as if he'd just said something clever.

Susie smiled. The boys groaned.

Mystified by everyone's behavior, Mary hung back. Greg came up beside her. "You look kinda . . . strange," he said. "Like you just lost your best friend."

Mary smiled at him. *He* was her best friend. It was reassuring just to have him nearby. She wanted to ask him what he thought of Susie and whether he'd noticed any change in their classmates, but now was not the time nor the place. Besides, she might be imagining the whole thing.

Everybody acts a little different in the presence of a stranger. Perhaps she was detecting change only because she was expecting it. "Nothing," she said. "Did you study for the test?"

Greg hit his forehead with the heel of his hand. "The test!" he said. "I forgot all about it."

The word *test!* traveled through the line with the swiftness of a current through a wire.

Several people turned panicked eyes on Mary. Susie was one of them. As her big sister, Mary felt duty-bound to put her at ease.

"Tell Susie not to worry," she said to Danny Doucette, who was in front of her.

He just stared at her, his green eyes blank.

"Pass it on, Danny," Mary urged. "Mrs. Anson won't expect her to take the test." She had a feeling Mrs. Anson wouldn't give the test at all this afternoon. She was about to say so when Amy asked, "What test?"

"Grammar," Mary answered, "But — "

"Who told you we were having a test, Mags?" Marisa asked.

"Mrs. Anson," Mary said. "Who else?"

"When?" Richard said. Wet splotches dotted the front of his plaid shirt, and he smelled of milk. "I don't remember anything about a test."

"She told us last week."

"Last week!" Amy said.

"Serve her right if everyone fails," Tommy said.

"Right," Matt put in. "How can anyone remember something as stupid as a test that long?"

"Mrs. Anson said we have to get used to the idea," Mary reminded them. "She said sometimes in junior high we'll get assignments for the whole week or even a month. You're supposed to write them down in your assignment book."

"Who needs an assignment book with you around to remind us, Mags?" Tommy said.

"I didn't remind anybody about anything," Mary said. "I wasn't even talking to any of you. I was talking to Greg!"

"Yeah," Greg chimed in. "She wasn't even talking to you guys. She was talking to me."

The line began to move.

"And besides, Mrs. Anson's not even going to give the test today," Mary said.

"Who says?" Matt asked.

"I have a — "

" — feeling," everyone finished.

Susie cocked her head and stared at Mary in a funny way, almost as if Mary were a creature from another planet.

Oh, great! Mary thought. That's all she needed was another person to make fun of her psychic feelings. Averting her eyes, she untucked her hair from behind her ear.

When the class was settled in their seats, Mrs. Anson said, "I promised you a grammar test this afternoon."

Heads turned toward Mary. Writing her name in the right-hand corner of a clean sheet of notebook paper, she pretended not to notice.

Amy muttered, "You and your *feelings*."

Mary pressed down on her pencil point. It snapped.

"But I'm postponing it," Mrs. Anson continued.

The class breathed a collective sigh of relief. But no one looked at Mary. She wasn't surprised. They were quick to tease her when she was wrong, but they rarely gave her credit when she was right.

Mrs. Anson walked towards the window. "We have something more important to deal with this afternoon."

The violets! Mary thought.

When everyone but Susie sank down in their seats and cast accusing glances at Amy, she knew they were all thinking the same thing.

Mrs. Anson turned to the class. Her forehead creased. "What is this?" she asked. "Slouch city?" She smiled at Susie as if to apologize to her for the class' behavior. Still, no one moved until she said firmly, "I'd appreciate your full attention."

Everyone sat up straight.

"That's better," Mrs. Anson said. Then with a flourish, she turned to the blackboard and wrote S-C-I-E-N-C-E F-A-I-R.

An astonished murmur broke over the room.

"That's what we're going to talk about?" Tommy asked.

Mrs. Anson nodded. "I know you were expecting the fair to take place sometime in spring, but there's been a scheduling conflict and it's been moved up. We have only six weeks to prepare."

"That's a long time," someone said.

"It may seem so," Mrs. Anson said, "but it'll go by quickly. I hope everyone will participate." She went on talking about the fair, outlining the steps to follow. Finally she said, "What I want you to do now is make a list of possible projects." Over the sounds of notebook rings opening and closing, paper tearing, feet shuffling, she added, "Choose two or three things that interest you and write them down."

"Can we work with somebody?" Marisa asked.

"Yes," Mrs. Anson answered, "but not now. I want each of you to make a list. We'll compare them later and, on the basis of common interest, we'll decide on teams." She glanced at Susie. "Were there science fairs at your other school?"

Susie stood up. "Yes," she said, "but only the kids who were good in science were in them."

Mrs. Anson nodded. "That's another advantage of a small school," she said. "Everyone has a chance." She smiled. "If you need any help, you just say so."

Tommy shot to his feet. "I'll help her, Mrs. Anson," he offered.

That was so unlike Tommy. He had never before indicated an interest in girls — except as objects of his teasing. None of the boys had.

Even Mrs. Anson looked surprised. "Thank you, Tommy," she said. "But I'm sure Mary Agnes can answer Susie's questions."

Susie flashed Mary a grateful smile.

Looking disappointed, Tommy sat down.

"Now, let's get to work," the teacher directed.

The noisy undercurrent trickled down to murmuring.

Mary glanced around the room. People were bent over their papers or staring out the windows. Marisa's foot swung in circles. Richard hummed. Laurie tapped her pencil on her desk. Mrs. Anson ambled up one aisle and down another, glancing at a paper here, making a suggestion there. Seemingly unaware of the distractions, Susie was hunched over her desk, her left arm protecting her paper.

Mary sighed. Usually she, too, could shut out everything and concentrate on the task at hand, but not this afternoon. Her mind kept skipping from one thing to another: Susie's arrival this morning; her own mixed feelings about her role as big sister; Tommy's uncharacteristic offer of help; Amy's two-faced behavior; her premonition that the sixth grade was about to change. . . .

She pushed herself up with her arms and tucked a leg under her. She got out another pencil — her last sharpened pencil — and retraced her name and the date at the top of her paper. *Science Project*, she printed at the center of the first line. She skipped a line and wrote, *Volcanoes*, immediately erasing it. She'd done that last year.

The clock above the blackboards clicked and the big hand jumped forward.

Mary stared at Greg, hoping to get his attention. Maybe he'd give her an idea, but he was sitting sideways, his back to her.

She sighed again.

"Ssshhh," Richard hissed.

She shot him a tight-lipped glance. He was the one making all the noise.

He grinned at her and resumed his humming.

"Sssssshhhhhh!" Mary said.

Nearly every head turned to aim a dirty look her way.

Mrs. Anson kept Susie after school.

Mary was glad. It meant she didn't have to hang around playing big sister and miss the chance to walk home with Greg.

"I'm sure glad Mrs. Anson didn't collect the science papers," she said to him as they crossed the street.

"Me, too," Greg said.

Mary was surprised. "Couldn't you think of anything either?"

"I had too much!" he said. "She told us two or three things; I had ten!"

"Really?" Mary's voice was full of admiration. "Like what?"

"Weather and time and space and — "

"Those are pretty general," Mary said. "I mean *weather* — that's a pretty big subject."

"She didn't say we had to narrow it down, Mags. Just list what interested us."

"But you can't work on *weather* unless it's one thing like tornadoes or something."

Greg said, "Whatever," and hopped up onto a low rock retaining wall where he did a couple of *t'ai chi* moves.

"You'd better get down," Mary cautioned. "Mrs. Popek is probably watching you."

Pretending the wall was a narrow ledge, Greg put one foot directly in front of the other as he moved along.

"You know she doesn't like people on her wall. She's afraid you'll fall into her flowers."

"Do I ever fall?"

"Still," Mary said. "She doesn't like to see people on the wall."

"Then she shouldn't watch," Greg said. He jumped down beside her. "One of these days, Mags, I'm going to get you to walk it, too."

Mary doubted it. She often thought about taking the kind of risks Greg did, but she could never bring herself to do it.

Referring to the science projects, Greg said, "You weren't the only one who couldn't think of anything. Susie's paper was blank, too."

Mary's eyes snapped toward him. She had wanted to bring up the subject of Susie, but she hadn't known exactly what to say. This gave her an opening. "How'd you know?"

"I saw her paper. It was blank — she didn't even have her name on it."

Remembering how Susie had hunched over her paper as if it were a treasure, Mary asked, "How'd you do that? See her paper?"

Greg shrugged. "I looked over her shoulder."

Mary nodded. In all the time Amy had sat in front of him, Greg had never once looked over her shoulder. It was just as Mary had predicted: Things were changing. And Susie Marsden was the cause.

5

Her leg tucked up under her, Mary was studying the spelling list at the round kitchen table when the phone rang. Thinking it was Nina wanting to get her opinion of Susie, Mary said, "I knew you'd call."

There was a pause, and then a voice said, "You did?"

It was Susie!

Mary unfolded her leg. "Oh, hi," Mary said. "Sorry about that."

"Oh, I think it's . . . awesome," Susie said.

Awesome? Mary repeated silently. She hadn't the slightest idea what Susie was referring to.

"Mrs. Anson gave me your number," Susie went on. "She said you'd give me the spelling list. I won't get my books for a few days and — " Susie chuckled. "But why am I telling you? You probably already know all that."

Mary wondered how she could possibly know

any of that, but she didn't say so. Instead she asked, "Got a pencil?"

"Uh-huh," Susie answered.

"The first word is *receive,*" she said. "R-e-c-e-i-v-e."

There was a long pause during which Mary could hear Susie breathing.

"Got it?" Mary asked.

"I think so," Susie said.

Mary went through the list slowly. After the last word, she said, "That's it. The test is tomorrow afternoon. Spelling tests are always on Tuesday afternoons."

"Mrs. Anson told me," Susie said. "When do you think she'll collect the science paper?"

"The project list? She'll let us know ahead of time."

"I couldn't think of a thing."

"I know," Mary said and instantly regretted it. Now, Susie would ask her how she knew.

But Susie didn't ask. Instead, she said, "Oh, right," without a trace of surprise in her voice.

This is the strangest conversation, Mary thought. After a long pause, she said, "Good luck on the spelling test."

"Thanks," Susie said. Adding, "See you tomorrow," she hung up.

The phone rang again. This time it was Nina.

"What'dya think of Susie?" she asked.

Mary twisted the yellow phone cord around her finger. "I just talked to her."

"You did? Did you call her or what?"

"I don't even know her number," Mary said. "She called me for the spelling list."

"What'd you talk about?"

"You mean after I gave her the words? Not much. It was a real strange conversation. Half the time, I didn't know what she was talking about," Mary said.

"Did she say what she's going to wear tomorrow?" Nina asked.

"No. Why?"

"A dress, is she going to wear a dress again?" Nina persisted.

"I don't know, Nina. I just told you, we didn't talk about clothes. I gave her the spelling list. She doesn't have her books yet."

"Do you think she will?"

"What?"

"Wear a dress," Nina said impatiently. "I think she will, don't you? I mean if she didn't change at lunch . . . ."

Nina's interest in Susie's clothes baffled Mary, but she went along with her. "She probably didn't have time to change or she thought it'd look funny if she did," she said. "But she'll wear something different tomorrow."

"You're probably right." Nina sounded satisfied.

Finally, Mary thought, we're done with the subject of clothes!

Then, Nina asked, "What're you going to wear tomorrow, Mags?"

"I knew it!" Nina said next morning as she and Mary approached school. "She's wearing a dress!"

Mary followed her friend's gaze. Susie Marsden was standing at the far corner of the playground near the basketball hoop in the same dress she'd worn yesterday.

"Maybe she doesn't have anything else," Mary said.

Amy came running up to join them. "Did you see what she's wearing?"

"She called Mags last night," Nina informed the gathering group.

Laurie glared at Mary. "Well, you could've told us at least!"

"Called us or something," Jennifer agreed.

"For what?" Mary asked.

"To tell us she was wearing a dress," Amy said.

Mary sighed. "I didn't know she was wearing a dress."

Marisa appeared. "Would you believe who she's talking to?" she asked.

Beside Susie, Tommy was passing a basketball from one hand to the other.

The girls knotted near the front door. They watched in amazement as, one by one, the boys sauntered over to Susie and Tommy. Before long, Susie was surrounded.

"I can't see," Laurie said. "What's she doing?"

Jennifer, the tallest person in the class, moved up two steps for a better view. "Smiling," she said.

"That's all she ever does," Marisa put in.

"To show off her dimples," Amy said.

"Now, she's talking," Jennifer observed.

"Boy crazy," Amy said.

"That's for sure," Marisa agreed, but her voice was full of admiration.

Suddenly, Tommy tossed the ball to Matt, who threw it toward the basketball hoop. The boys scattered across the court, leaving Susie standing alone.

Amy turned her back. "Pretend we don't see her," she said.

"Why?" Mary asked.

"She likes the boys, doesn't she?"

Mary didn't see the connection. She was about to ask Amy to explain, when Marisa broke from the group and skipped over to Susie.

Everyone else followed.

"You got here early," Amy said to Susie. It sounded like an accusation.

Looking Amy straight in the eye, Susie said, "Yes."

Mary liked that. If she had been Susie, she would have given a long, boring explanation.

"Did you bring any candy?" Laurie asked.

Susie smiled. "No, but I will if you want me to."

"What did you and the boys talk about?" Marisa asked.

Susie shrugged. "Nothing much," she said. "They were just being nice."

Saying "Nice," Jennifer shook her head.

"How come you wore a dress?" Nina asked.

"I like dresses," Susie said.

The bell rang.

Amy took Susie's arm. "Come on, Susie," she said. "I'll be your partner."

Marisa pushed in between them. "You were her partner yesterday, Amy."

Amy's hands flew to her sides. "So what?"

"We should take turns," Laurie said as she took Susie's other arm.

"Right," Jennifer said. "It's my turn." Jennifer and Laurie turned to face each other.

Susie backed away from the argument and joined Mary on the sidelines. The two of them walked, side by side, to the sixth-grade line.

6

All morning, Mrs. Anson was full of energy, smiling and making jokes, stopping now and then beside Susie to be sure she was keeping up. Susie responded with polite, dimpled smiles, and soft replies.

Everyone else was on their best behavior, too. People who rarely answered in class waved their hands to be recognized, and everyone remembered to stand up when called on without being reminded.

Mary, usually one of the first with the answers, didn't have the chance to recite at all. After a while, she didn't even bother to raise her hand.

Mrs. Anson didn't seem to notice. Instead, she commented favorably and often on everyone's participation and on the amount the class was accomplishing as a result.

* * *

Susie went home for lunch again.

Still, she was present in the girls' minds as they took their usual table near the door of the gym. They were all so quiet it was as if the new girl had cast a spell over them.

Attempting to bring them back to themselves, Mary said what she had said yesterday, "I can't wait till next year when we have a real cafeteria."

No one responded.

"I just can't wait," she repeated. She glanced at her friends expectantly, waiting for the customary responses.

Nina was pressing a forefinger into her cheek.

Amy was scrutinizing her Reeboks.

At the end of the table, Jennifer and Laurie were examining their sandwiches as if they thought they might be poisoned.

Across the room, even the boys seemed strange. They were eating their lunches in slow motion, sappy looks in their eyes. And Greg — of all people! — was acting as dopey as the rest of them.

"What's wrong with everybody?" Mary asked.

"What isn't?" Nina responded.

"I think I need a new pair of shoes," Amy said.

"You just got those last week," Mary reminded her.

Amy shrugged. "Yeah, well, things change."

"That's for sure," Mary agreed.

"At least you can *buy* shoes," Nina put in.

Everyone nodded. Except Mary. She had never seen her friends act like this. Except for Greg and Marisa, the class had been together since kindergarten. They had shared much, but nothing had ever affected them like this.

"What's that supposed to mean?" she asked, knowing the answer.

"Nina means you only get one face," Jennifer explained.

"And one body," Laurie added.

"What I think we should do," Amy announced, glancing around the table to be sure she had everyone's attention, "is . . . ignore her."

"And what?" Mary scoffed. "She'll just go away?"

Jennifer's dark eyes flashed with excitement. "You know, she might. I mean if she doesn't like it here, maybe her parents'll transfer her or move away or something."

Mary pulled the corners of her mouth back into her most effective *I-can't-believe-this!* expression.

"Mary's got them just like her!" Nina exclaimed. She mimicked Mary's expression.

Jennifer and Laurie copied Nina.

Amy leaned close to inspect Mary's face. "Those are just . . . creases," she said.

The other girls relaxed their faces.

"What are we *talking* about?" Mary asked.

"You know," Nina said impatiently.

Mary pulled her hair forward to cover her ears. "I guess we're talking about . . . dimples," she admitted. "I just don't know *why*."

"Because we don't have them and *she* does," Nina said.

Jennifer sighed. "And she's so . . . tiny."

"You always liked being the tallest per — " Mary stopped herself from saying *person*. Something told her Jennifer wouldn't like that distinction today. " — girl."

"That was before," Jennifer said.

"Who says dimples are so great?" Mary asked. "I mean we're acting like she's something special and we don't even know her." No one responded. "You know what Mrs. Anson always says," she added.

Everyone knew. Mrs. Anson always said that what counted was on the inside: a good heart and a curious mind.

Remembering that seemed to make everyone feel better until Nina said, "What if she has those, too?"

7

That afternoon, a brief tension temporarily altered the mood during the spelling test when Mrs. Anson, who always ambled up and down the aisles as she dictated the words, hesitated beside her African violets.

In the long silence that followed, Mary had the urge to spring to her feet and confess. When heads turned in her direction, issuing mute warnings, she decided to remain silent.

Trying to concentrate on her spelling paper, she retraced the numbers before each word, re-crossed her *t*'s, and re-dotted her *i*'s.

Finally, Mrs. Anson turned back to the class. "*Deceit*," she pronounced. "An honest person does not deal in *deceit*."

Expecting the woman's eyes to be focused on her accusingly, Mary cast a furtive glance in her direction.

Mrs. Anson smiled. "That one shouldn't give

you any trouble," she said. "Just remember the rule."

I before *e* except after *c*, Mary recited silently, but her hand did not obey her mind. In her hurry to correct the misspelled word, she broke her pencil. Her last pencil.

Mrs. Anson stacked the collected papers on her desk. Then, with a glance at the clock, she announced, "We have some time this afternoon for creative writing. Please get out your composition books, and, remember, first drafts are always done in pencil."

Mary whispered, "Can I borrow a pencil?" across to Greg.

Before he could respond, Susie turned in her seat and presented Mary with a freshly sharpened lavender pencil. And a smile.

"Thanks," Mary said, "but you might need it."

Susie shook her head. "I have a whole bunch." She held up a clear plastic box filled with pencils, pens, and other equipment. "They have my name on them."

At the blackboard, Mrs. Anson stopped giving instructions and focused on Mary. "Is there a problem, Mary Agnes?"

Mary shot to her feet. "Not exactly," she said. "I broke a pencil yesterday when we were doing the science project list and I forgot to sharpen it.

44

Then I broke my last one during spelling so I asked Greg if I could borrow one" — Greg pulled at the edge of her red cardigan. She knew he was trying to tell her to be quiet, but she couldn't seem to stop. — "but Susie said I could have one of hers" — Tommy dropped his head to his desk and pretended to have fallen asleep — "but I thought she might need it so I said — "

"Do you have a pencil now, Mary Agnes?" Mrs. Anson interrupted.

Mary shifted from one foot to the other. "Well, no, because — "

Five hands reached out toward her, each holding a pencil.

Mary hesitated, not knowing which one to accept.

Greg grabbed them all and dropped them on her desk.

"That should take care of the problem," Mrs. Anson concluded and turned back to the board. "In the time remaining, I want each of you to write a story using these — "

The bell rang.

Mrs. Anson sighed. "Be sure you all have sharpened pencils tomorrow," she said.

Usually, someone would have teased Mary about her habit of giving long explanations when asked a question, especially by anyone in authority. But today, no one said a word. Instead, they all crowded around Susie's desk.

Mary was relieved. And disappointed.

"Wait up!" Greg called.

At the corner, Mary stopped and turned. Greg came loping towards her, his bookbag slung over one shoulder.

"What's your hurry?" he asked as he approached.

Mary had left school quickly without stopping to talk to Susie as everyone else had.

Mary shrugged. "No hurry."

"You sure disappeared fast." It sounded like an accusation.

"I didn't *disappear;* I just . . . left." Mary resumed walking.

Greg said, "Whatever," and hopped up onto Mrs. Popek's retaining wall. Seeing the woman in the window, he jumped back down.

"How'd you do on the spelling test?" Mary asked.

Greg shrugged. "Probably flunked. How can anybody keep all those *i-e*'s straight."

"You just have to remember the rule," Mary said.

"And all the exceptions."

"There aren't that many."

"It's all pretty stupid if you ask me. Spelling," he scoffed. "Who cares?"

"If you can't spell, Greg, what will you do when you grow up?"

"Hire a secretary," Greg said.

"Someone like Susie Marsden?" Mary teased, surprising herself. She had had no intention of bringing up Susie's name.

"Naw. She probably can't spell either."

Now that the subject of Susie was out in the open, Mary decided to pursue it. "So what do you think of her?" she asked, trying not to sound too interested.

"What do *you* think of her?"

"I asked first," Mary objected.

"I think you don't like her," Greg said.

"I didn't ask you what *I* think, Greg."

"Well, do you?"

"How do I know? I mean I don't even *know* her."

"You're never going to get to know her if you keep running away."

Mary halted abruptly. Her hands flew to her hips. "I did not run away." The teasing twinkle in Greg's dark eyes made her feel silly. Murmuring, "Oh, Greg," she swatted at him with her hand. "Why do you tease me all the time?"

He danced away, laughing. "Because you make it so easy."

"Very funny," she said. "Besides, how can anybody get to know anybody with everybody trying to get to know somebody?"

"It *was* kind of a crowd," Greg agreed.

"I suppose Marisa asked her over," Mary said.

"*Every*body asked her over." He paused. "I take that back. Laurie asked if she could go to Susie's house."

Mary nodded. "Because of the candy." She turned her head to look at him. "I don't think that's any reason to like somebody, do you? Because their mother makes candy?"

Greg shrugged. "It's no reason not to like them."

Mary had to admit he was right about that. She glanced at him and then looked quickly away. "How come you didn't stay with everybody else?"

Greg bent over and picked up a stone. "The whole scene was getting ridiculous," he said as he tossed it in the air. "Matt and Tommy actually got into this big thing about who was going to carry Susie's books."

"She didn't have any books," Mary said.

Greg smiled. "I told you, the whole thing was stupid."

"How'd Susie react?"

"She just kept smiling," Greg said, "but I think she's smart enough to know what's going on."

That was more than Mary knew. She glanced at Greg out of the corner of her eye. "You think she's smart?"

"Smart enough."

"For what?"

Greg shook his head. "I don't know for what — for anything!"

"School?" Mary persisted. "You just said she probably can't sp — "

"Don't worry, Mags, you'll still be the smartest," Greg interrupted, an amused edge to his voice.

"Oh, I didn't mean . . ." her voice trailed off. She didn't know what she meant. "It was such a . . . crazy day. Everybody was so strange. Nobody acted like that when you first came to Merredith Heights."

Greg stopped in his tracks. "That's for sure. Nobody paid any attention to me at all. It was like I was invisible."

"I was nice to you," Mary reminded him.

Greg's wide, warm smile spilled into his eyes. "You were the only one," he said. "It was a coupla weeks before anyone but you even talked to me unless they had to."

"All Susie did was walk into the room and

everybody wants to be her friend." Mary thought about the difference in the class' attitude for several seconds before adding, "It's probably because we were so young then."

"I don't think that's the reason," Greg said seriously.

Mary shot him an inquisitive glance.

He met her eyes. "I think it's because," he paused, a lopsided grin belying his solemn tone, "I don't have dimples."

Mary groaned. *"Dimples!* That's all anybody wants to talk about. Nina actually tried to drill some into her face!"

Greg laughed. "It's no big deal, Mary," he said. "In a coupla days, Susie'll just be another sixth grader, and everybody'll go back to being their obnoxious selves."

Although Mary thought everyone was being obnoxious now, she knew what Greg meant. "I hope you're right," she said.

8

At home, Mary called Nina. They had had plans to stop at Sweet 'n' Ice, the yogurt restaurant, after school, but with all the commotion over Susie, Mary had decided not to wait. Now she felt bad. It wasn't like her to leave as she had without a word to Nina. She had to apologize. Maybe there was still time to meet her friend at the mall.

Nina wasn't home. "They all went over to the new girl's house," Mrs. Ross told Mary.

Mary sat on the high stool by the phone in the kitchen for a long time. There were so many feelings whirling around inside her, she didn't have the energy to move. How could Nina do this? And without even calling!

Mrs. Gardner came into the kitchen, a wash basket in her arms. "Hi, Sweetie," she said. "How was your day?"

51

"Weird," Mary told her.

"The new girl?" her mother asked.

Mary was surprised. She hadn't told her mother about Susie. "You know about that?" she said.

Mrs. Gardner nodded. "Nina told me."

"She called?" Mary hopped off the stool. "She leave a message or anything?"

"She said everyone'd be at the new girl's house if you wanted to meet them there."

Mary sighed heavily. Obviously, Nina had forgotten all about their plans.

"You and Nina had plans," her mother said as though she had read her daughter's thoughts.

Mary nodded. "I suppose it's as much my fault as Nina's," she admitted. "I should've stayed, but everyone was acting so weird."

Mrs. Gardner shifted the wash basket to one arm and crossed to the basement stairs. "New broom," she said as though that explained everything.

Mary didn't understand. "What?"

Her mother set the wash basket on the top step. "It's an expression my mother always used," she answered. " 'A new broom sweeps clean.' "

"What's that have to do with anything?" Mary asked.

"In this case, it means relax. In a day or two

52

the new girl'll be just one of the group."

Mary smiled. "You mean she'll be an old broom just like the rest of us?"

Her mother laughed. "You've got the idea," she said.

Nina's phone was busy all evening. So was Marisa's and Laurie's and Jennifer's and Amy's. Finally, Mary phoned Greg.

"You should've come over to Susie's," he said.

Mary couldn't believe her ears. "You went there, too?"

"Everyone was there." He sounded defensive.

"I wasn't," Mary said, realizing immediately how dumb it sounded. He already knew she hadn't been there.

"Except you," he amended. "Why didn't you come?"

"For one thing, I don't even know where she lives." *And I don't care*, she added silently.

"Oleander," Greg said. "The Bartons' old house."

"Did you have a good time?"

"It was okay," Greg said. "We watched Susie's mother make candy. She's got this big marble slab in the kitchen and she — "

"What'd Susie do?"

"She wasn't home."

Mary repeated, "She wasn't home," to be sure

she had heard correctly, then she began to giggle. "She wasn't even home?"

On the other end of the line, Greg chortled. "I guess it is kinda funny."

His understatement made Mary laugh harder. Greg joined in. Before long they were both laughing so hard they couldn't talk.

9

A rusty van pulled up at the curb.

"Hi, Mary," Susie called from the open window. "Want a ride?"

Mary hesitated, not knowing what to say. She liked to walk, but she didn't want to hurt Susie's feelings by refusing the ride. "I — uh — " she began uncertainly.

Susie said something to her father and hopped out of the van. She was wearing a dress; colorful flowers sprinkled on a yellow background. Too lightweight for fall, Mary thought, but still, it looked nice on Susie.

"Let's walk," Susie said as she joined Mary on the sidewalk. "That way we can talk."

Mary nodded.

Susie smiled. Even her dimples seemed less obvious this morning. "Do you always walk?" she asked.

"Most of the time," Mary answered.

"I couldn't walk to my old school. It was too far. I had to take the school bus," Susie said. "I hated it." She turned her head to look at Mary. "Alone?"

Mary knew what she meant. "Sometimes I walk with Greg Hopkins and sometimes I meet someone, Nina or someone, along the way."

"Greg seems really nice," Susie said.

Mary didn't know what to say, so she said, "I like to walk. Especially in the morning. It sorta wakes me up. Gets me ready for school."

Laughing, Susie said, "Nothing could get *me* ready for *school*."

Mary laughed, too. She liked school so much that she never believed those who said they didn't. She figured they only said it to make an impression.

"It's not that I don't *like* it," Susie went on. "It's just that I'm not very . . . good at it."

"I'll bet you are," Mary said, remembering how attentive Susie had been in class.

"No, really, I'm not."

Mary shrugged. Who was she to argue?

They walked along in silence until Susie said, "I was sorry I wasn't home yesterday when you all came over."

Mary opened her mouth to say she hadn't been there, then decided against it. "Where were you?"

"Paul — he's my brother; he goes to high school — took me back to the old neighborhood to see my friend Nicky."

Mary wondered if Nicky was a boy or a girl, but she didn't ask. Susie didn't leave space for any questions.

"It's really strange, going back like that. We went by our old house. The people who bought it are remodeling it. The whole front was torn off already. Paul says that's a good thing. Otherwise — if it looked the same — it'd be harder. I don't know, though. I hate to think of people tearing it apart like that."

Mary thought about her own house. She had been born there. She wondered how she would feel if some strangers took over and started changing everything. She couldn't imagine it. She had a hard time adjusting when her mother changed the wallpaper. "I like things to stay the same," she said.

"Some things," Susie agreed.

As they turned up the school walk, Mary stopped abruptly.

The girls were knotted on the front steps. They were all wearing dresses! Except Amy, who was in her best slacks.

Susie followed her gaze. Then, she turned questioning eyes on Mary.

"They're wearing dresses!" Mary explained.

"Oh," Susie said, but she obviously didn't understand Mary's surprise.

As the other girls scrambled toward them, the boys headed them off, crowding around Susie.

Unnoticed, Mary drifted out of the circle to join her complaining classmates.

"It's not fair." Marisa's black hair bounced as she bobbed her head for emphasis. "She should talk to us, not the boys."

"I told you she's just boy crazy," Amy put in smugly.

Mary glanced toward the boys. Tommy and Matt's voices rose as they vied with each other for Susie's attention. The others urged them on or grinned silently at Susie. At the center, Susie stood smiling sweetly.

"No wonder I couldn't get her on the phone last night," Nina said. "She was probably talking to one of *them*." She jerked a thumb over her shoulder towards the boys.

"Her line was busy all night," Laurie confirmed.

Mary was irritated. Obviously, no one had bothered to phone *her* last night. And that's why she hadn't been able to get through to any of them! Their attitude towards Susie annoyed her, too. Only yesterday, she might have agreed that Susie was boy crazy, but this morning, she wasn't so

58

sure. Susie hadn't invited any of this attention, and, no matter how sweetly she smiled, she seemed uncomfortable with it. Mary had a sudden urge to defend the girl. "Your lines were all busy, too," she accused. "Were you talking to one of *them*?"

Amy turned on her. "On second thought," she said, "maybe you were the one talking to her."

"Right," Jennifer concurred.

"Is that why you didn't call me?" Nina asked.

Mary sighed. "I did call!" she said. "I just told you I called everybody!"

Amy said, "So you did talk to her," as she glanced around the group smugly.

"I didn't say that!" Mary protested.

But no one was listening. They had turned their attention to Susie.

"Look at her," Amy scoffed.

Marisa looked down at her plaid dress. "How come none of the boys are talking to us?"

"That's what I want to know," Laurie said. "We wore dresses, too."

"It's because she's boy crazy," Jennifer said.

The conversation was making Mary dizzy. "I give up!" she muttered and stalked off. At the door, she looked back. Susie was skipping towards her. Crowding around Susie, the girls cut her off.

One minute they were calling Susie names and

the next they were jostling one another to get close to her! Mary shook her head.

"What's happening?" Greg asked as he came outside.

"Beats me," Mary said.

10

The events of the morning didn't help to clear Mary's confusion. People found excuses to pass by Susie's desk and drop notes. The new girl accepted each with a shy smile and, when no one was looking, tucked it into her pencil box without reading it.

Mary sat back and watched in disbelief. Her classmates, people she had known forever, were suddenly strangers. Susie, too, was a puzzlement. On the way to school, she had been open and talkative. Here, in the classroom, she was a different person, shy, almost withdrawn.

During the last period before lunch, Mrs. Anson asked Susie to read. It was the first time since her arrival that she had been called on. An expectant silence fell over the class as though it were an audience waiting for the show to begin.

The color drained from Susie's face as she got

to her feet. Biting her lower lip, she adjusted the reader in her hands.

The clock on the wall above the blackboards measured the passing seconds in clicks and whirrs; otherwise, there was no sound.

"Susie?" Mrs. Anson said at last.

Susie started. "Yes, Mrs. Anson?" she said softly.

"Have you lost the place?"

Dropping her gaze to the book, Susie shook her head slightly and took a deep breath. Then, in a small, halting voice, she began to read.

The fire drill bell sounded.

Susie's whole body relaxed, and Mary wouldn't have been surprised to hear her say, "Saved by the bell."

"Line up by rows," Mrs. Anson directed.

Everyone scrambled out of their chairs.

"Quickly. Quietly," the teacher reminded them. She threw open the door and marched out, leading the way to the nearest exit.

Behind her, people jockeyed for positions close to Susie, but Greg, who was behind her, held his ground.

By the time the class had found its place on the playground, Mary was at the end of the line. She stood shivering in the fall air feeling left out and lonely.

Mrs. Anson began a head count while they waited for the signal to return to their classroom. "This is the sloppiest line I've ever seen," she said. "I can't tell who's here and who isn't." She waved her hands, palms parallel, as though she were straightening a stack of papers.

The class instantly fell into a more orderly line.

"Where's Christopher?" the teacher asked.

Everyone looked around for Christopher Carey, the smallest person in the class.

His curly head bobbed up between Jennifer and Tommy. "Here!" he called out and disappeared again.

Mrs. Anson waved him forward. "Come up here where I can see you, Christopher," she said. "Let's all line up according to height."

That kind of line was Mrs. Anson's favorite. Mary liked it, too. It meant that Greg was always right behind her. Smiling, she slid in between him and Susie.

"Susie's taller than you, Mary," Amy said from her place near the front of the line.

Mary pulled a face. Why couldn't Amy mind her own business? "She is not!"

Everyone stepped out of line and stood back to measure.

"Mrs. Anson," Amy persisted, "isn't Susie taller than Mary?"

Several yards away, conferring with another teacher, Mrs. Anson didn't respond.

Jennifer put a hand on each girl's shoulder. "Turn around, you two."

Mary stiffened. "I will not turn around," she objected. But she did.

When Jennifer was satisfied that both girls were standing correctly, back to back, heels down, she bridged their heads with an open palm. "Susie's taller," she announced.

Mary's hand flew to her head. Susie did seem taller by a fraction — too small a fraction to justify a change. Mary belonged near Greg. It was her place. It had been her place since fourth grade. "Her hair's higher than mine," Mary said. "Hers is curly, and mine is flat. That's the only difference."

Amy shook her head. "It has nothing to do with hair," she said.

Mary looked to Greg, certain he'd back her up.

Avoiding Mary's eyes, he confirmed, "Susie's taller."

"Told you," Jennifer said and pushed Susie into line.

Susie whispered, "Sorry," into Mary's ear, but that didn't change the fact that she was now between Mary and Greg.

*   *   *

Back in the classroom, Mrs. Anson lectured on the seriousness of fire drills. "We were the worst class," she said. "Slowest. Noisiest. Most disorderly. Totally unacceptable." She excused Susie, whose father was waiting to take her home for lunch, and made the rest of the class line up by rows again. "You're the oldest in the school," she admonished them. "You must set a good example." She led them outside and back in, repeating the entire process until she was satisfied with their behavior. By the time she released them, there was little time for lunch.

On the way to the gym, Greg joked, "She's so worried about a fire, she'll starve us to death."

"It was all Mary's fault we had to go through all that," Amy put in.

A hot rush of anger flooded Mary. "*My* fault? How was it my fault?"

"If you'd just let Susie in line behind you instead of making a big scene about it," Amy said.

Mary's mouth dropped open in disbelief. She tried to defend herself, but all that came out was a series of sputters.

She looked to Greg to rescue her, but he had dashed on ahead to join the other boys.

Laurie, who had stopped at the girls' room, caught up to the group as they took their places at the table. "How'd you like *reading*?" she asked, raising an eyebrow meaningfully.

Jennifer chortled. "I never thought she'd get through the first sentence."

"She didn't!" Laurie said. "That's what I mean."

"Do you suppose . . ?" Jennifer shook her head as though to clear away the thought.

But Amy scooped it up. "She can *read*," she said. "It's part of her act."

Nina's round face crinkled with the effort of understanding. "What act?"

"Her *poor-little-me* act, that's what act."

There was a long silence while everyone thought about that.

Finally, Nina said, "I don't get it."

"She wants the boys to think she's helpless," Amy said.

"Why would she want to do that?" Jennifer asked.

"So they'll *help* her, why else?"

"Help her with what?" Laurie asked.

Amy rolled her eyes. "I don't mean *help* her exactly."

A light went on in Nina's eyes. "You mean she was . . . pretending she couldn't read?"

"Right," Amy said.

Nina's eyes clouded again. "I still don't get it."

"Why would anybody do that?" Jennifer asked.

"Boys like dumb girls," Amy said.

Nina wasn't convinced. "What'd you think, Mary?"

Mary's rapid change of emotion — from anger at Amy to disappointment with Greg — so absorbed her that she wasn't aware of the shift in the conversation. At the sound of her name, she murmured, "Why's everybody blaming me?"

Amy said, "Nobody's blaming you. Who said anything about blaming you?"

"You did, Amy. That's who." Mary crumpled her lunch bag. With tears stinging her eyes, she headed for the girls' room.

Nina came in at her heels. Her cheeks were flushed and she had a wild look in her eyes. "I can't believe what just happened!" she said.

Mary brushed away her tears with the back of her hand and smiled at her friend. She should've known Nina wouldn't let her down. Next to Greg, Nina was her best friend. She was always sensitive to people's feelings. Mary felt bad that she had been so quick to lump her with the others.

"Tommy held the door for me!" Nina danced in a circle. "We were coming out of the gym and he ran ahead to hold the door for me! And he actually smiled at me! Can you believe it?!" She rushed to the mirrors over the sinks and puffed up her cheeks. "My face is too round!"

Mary couldn't believe her ears. She stared at Nina, her tears forgotten.

"Maybe if I change my hair," Nina said, catching Mary's reflected eyes. "What do you think, Mary?"

Nina's short, dark blonde hair was soft and curly around her face. Swallowing hard, Mary said, "I like your hair."

Turning, Nina laughed. "I don't mean *that*! About *Tommy*! Do you have any . . . feelings — any *psychic* feelings — about Tommy and me? Do you think he . . . likes me?" She lowered her voice as though to keep the walls from hearing.

"No," Mary answered. "I don't have any feelings about that. I don't have any feelings about *anything*."

Mary suddenly remembered the conversation she and Susie had had on the way to school. It occurred to her that the sixth grade was like Susie's old house: a place she had once lived in comfortably. Now, however, some stranger had moved in and begun to remodel it. And Mary didn't know how to feel or what to do.

11

"Have you been thinking about your projects?" Mrs. Anson asked after lunch.

Everyone looked at her blankly.

"The science projects for the fair," she prompted.

Everyone nodded. "Yes, Mrs. Anson," they said.

"Good," she said. "Let's hear some of them." She raised an arm to let the class know she wanted volunteers. No one volunteered.

Mary sank down behind Christopher, but she knew Mrs. Anson would call on her anyway.

"Mary Agnes?"

Mary stood up. "I — uh — can't think of anything, Mrs. Anson," she said. From the corner of her eye, she saw Susie turn to look at her. Mary dropped her head forward, letting her hair fall over her ears.

"Keep thinking," the teacher said, "you'll come

up with something. But don't reach too far. The best ideas are right in front of us."

Mary wished she shared her teacher's confidence.

"Richard Bianchi?"

Richard shot to his feet, knocking his notebook to the floor.

"Is that a preview?" Mrs. Anson asked lightly. "Are you doing something on falling objects?"

Richard's eyes widened. "How'd you guess?" he asked as if he'd been planning all along to make that his project.

The class laughed. Everyone knew he'd just now gotten the idea.

Greg was next. "Weather," he said.

"That's too general," Mrs. Anson told him. "You'll have to narrow it down."

Mary shot him an *I-told-you-so* look.

Greg shrugged.

Mrs. Anson called on Amy.

"Volcanoes," she said.

Mary glared at her. Amy was copying her idea from last year, and it made her mad.

"Keep working," Mrs. Anson said to the class. "We'll talk more sometime in the next week or so."

"Are you going right home?" Mary asked Greg when the final bell rang. She was anxious to talk to him.

"I thought I'd hang around, see what the guys are doing," he answered. "Why?"

She shrugged. "No reason. I just thought" — Susie dropped her assignment notebook — "we could" — Greg leaned over and picked it up — "talk about the science projects, but . . ." her voice trailed off. She was wasting her breath. Greg wasn't listening. He was smiling sappily at Susie.

Tommy sauntered over. "Hey, Suz," he said. "Some of us are going to Sweet 'n' Ice. Wanna come along?"

Behind him, Nina glowered.

"Susie's coming over to my house," Marisa informed him.

"No, she isn't," Laurie said. "I'm going to her house."

"Who says?" Marisa challenged.

"She got my note first," Laurie answered. "Didn't you, Susie?"

Unnoticed, Mary slipped out of her chair and went to the coatroom. The long, narrow room smelled, as it always did, of sack lunches and chalk dust. Setting her books on the wooden floor, she grabbed her red sweater from her assigned hook. She stood by the door as she put it on, watching Susie, who sat calmly at her desk, while everyone argued around her. Sighing sadly, Mary picked up her books and started for home.

She was a block away when she heard running footsteps behind her. She glanced over her shoulder. "Susie!" she exclaimed, stopping in her tracks.

Susie pounded up beside her, laughing and breathless. "I never thought I'd catch up to you!" Her cheeks were rosy, and her blonde hair was windblown.

Mary squinted into the distance, expecting to see everyone else running along behind Susie. "Where is everybody?"

"Still arguing about who's doing what with whom," Susie said, her blue eyes twinkling. "They never even saw me leave!"

Serves 'em right, Mary thought.

"Are they always like that?" Susie asked. "I mean just because they write a person a note . . ."

"And you didn't even read them," Mary said.

Biting her lower lip, Susie flashed a guilty look. "You saw me?" Then she laughed. "I never read notes people send in class. Because if I do, then I have to answer them, and then I get caught. I'm the one who *always* gets caught."

"Really?" Mary said. She felt exactly the same way about herself, but she imagined Susie's looks and sweet manner would allow her to get away with anything.

Susie nodded. "And I have enough trouble in school without making it worse."

Mary said, "You seemed really nervous when Mrs. Anson called on you to read." Instantly, she wished she could take back her words.

But Susie wasn't the least disturbed by them. "I thought I'd throw up," she said, her tone matter-of-fact. "I hate reading out loud. Everything starts pounding in my ears and that's all I can think about."

Mary understood that. "I used to get real nervous, too," she said. "I still do get nervous, but not that bad anymore."

Susie's eyes widened with interest. They were the most incredible shade of blue Mary had ever seen. "How'd you get over it?"

"Well, I try to think of something else."

Susie groaned. "If I did that, I'd never understand what I'm reading."

"I don't mean I think of something else; I think about the words, but I don't think about reading them out loud in front of everybody."

"You mean you pretend you're somewhere else?"

"I don't think about the place at all."

"So you pretend you're . . . nowhere?"

Although Susie couldn't know it, she had just crystallized what Mary had been feeling: She *was*

73

nowhere. Hearing it eased the tension she'd been experiencing the last two days. She laughed. "I don't have to *pretend* that!" she said lightly.

Susie looked surprised. "You?" she said. "You should never feel like that. You're perfect, Mary. I wish I could be just like you."

The sincerity in her voice made Mary uncomfortable. She reached up and unhooked her hair from behind her left ear. "You don't know me," she objected, "or you wouldn't say that. You wouldn't ever say that."

"Oh, I know all kinds of things about you," Susie assured her. "You're smart and honest and nice." She smiled proudly. "My father says I'm very good at sizing people up." She slipped her arm through Mary's. "Can you come to my house for a while?"

Mary hesitated. "My mother expects me home," she said truthfully.

"You can call her from my house."

Mary thought about it. Anyone else in the class would have jumped at the invitation. But Susie was the reason she had been feeling so gloomy. On the other hand, Mary didn't have anything better to do. "Okay," she said at last. "Why not?"

12

Boxes stood around the Marsdens' living and dining rooms waiting to be unpacked.

"We've all been so busy . . . ," Susie explained as she led Mary through a swinging door into the kitchen.

This large, light room, by contrast to the others, seemed unusually neat and orderly. In the center was a large block. On top of that was a marble slab — the one Greg had mentioned. And the room smelled wonderful — all sweet and warm — like a candy store.

At the stove, stirring something in a big pot, a woman with a graying braid wrapped around her head smiled at the girls. Susie's mother.

"I'm going to show Mary the house," Susie said.

Her mother laughed. "I'm sure you'll like the decorating, Mary," she joked. "It's called early moving box."

Susie led the way through the kitchen to a little

hall where she opened a door. Stepping aside to let Mary enter, she said, "This is where we store the candy."

Mary squinted into the small room. She took a tentative step inside. It was so cold and dark she felt as though she were entering a giant refrigerator.

Saying, "Too much light and heat aren't good for candy," Susie snapped on the dim overhead light fixture.

Even then, Mary could barely make out the boxes on the shelves that lined the walls. "Those boxes aren't all filled with candy," she said. "They can't be!"

"They are," Susie assured her. She held out a box. "Want some?"

Mary's mouth watered at the sight of the chocolate mounds, and it was all she could do to keep from reaching out and snatching several from their white paper nests. "Won't your mother be mad?"

"The ones on this shelf," Susie indicated a bottom shelf, shorter than the others, next to the only window in the room, "are rejects."

Mary leaned close to the box. The chocolate aroma was so powerful it made her dizzy. "What's wrong with them?" she asked.

Susie shrugged. "Cracked or not the right shape — stuff like that."

"They look perfect to me," Mary said as she

lifted one from the box. She bit into the chocolate. A syrupy liquid ran down her chin. Laughing, she commented, "Cherry. My favorite."

"They're supposed to have a swirly *C* on top," Susie said as she glanced at the remaining pieces, "but with rejects, you can never tell." She pushed the box toward Mary. "Have some more."

"Aren't you going to have any?" Mary asked, remembering her manners just as her hand was about to dig in.

Susie shook her head. "I don't like candy."

Mary looked at her in disbelief. She thought Susie had said that yesterday only to put Laurie in her place.

"I used to," Susie continued, "when Mom was just starting to make it, before it was a business. When it's around all the time, you sorta lose your taste for it."

Mary doubted that would ever happen to her. "Are you sure it's okay to have more?" Susie nodded, so she took two more pieces. Maple. Vanilla. Her second and third favorites.

The telephone rang. Susie handed Mary the box and dashed out of the room to answer it.

Mary stared down at the box as though it were a trap she didn't know how to get out of. Finally, she took another piece, set the remainder on its shelf, and turned her back on it.

The words, "Oh, Nicky, am I glad you called!" drifted in to her.

Nicky, Susie's friend from the old school, Mary identified as she stepped out into the hall.

"I like it," Susie was saying. "Everybody's been real friendly, and I met this girl — Mary Agnes. Everybody calls her *Mags*, but I like *Mary* better. She's really nice."

Guilt rippled through Mary. Contrary to what Susie thought, she did not know Mary's true character.

Thinking that made Mary feel so awful that she decided she needed one more piece of candy. She slipped back into the room where she quickly snatched another piece and popped it into her mouth. Rum. Her least favorite. She held the box close looking for a swirly *C*. When she heard Susie coming into the hall, she grabbed the nearest piece. Orange. Her second to least favorite. I'm not very smart either, she chided herself, or I would have quit when I was ahead.

Upstairs, Susie's room was small. The light coming through the dormer windows was dingy, and the beige paint on the walls was peeling in spots. Packing boxes squatted in the corners or stood — half in, half out — of the small, open closet.

Susie hopped up onto the unmade bed. "Isn't it a neat room?" she said.

Mary didn't know what to say. Her own room was bright and cheerful and uncluttered. She had never seen it any other way. She would have a hard time getting used to this room. "I like the way the ceiling slants," she said at last.

"Me, too," Susie said. "I'm going to get wallpaper with tiny flowers all over it. Except here." She put her hands on the sloping ceiling to either side of her bed. "I think I'll get stripes or something for this part in the same colors."

"That'll look nice," Mary said. "Sort of like a canopy."

Susie jumped off the bed and went to the window alcove. "And we'll cover this radiator so I'll have a window seat."

Mary looked around the room. It did have possibilities, something she would never have seen without Susie.

Susie sat down on the radiator. "I was really surprised when you said you didn't have a science project," she said.

Mary shrugged. "Science isn't my favorite subject."

"But with your *feelings* and all," Susie said.

Mary couldn't imagine what psychic feelings had to do with science projects. She looked at-

Susie, a question in her eyes, but Susie had turned towards the windows.

"Oh, look!" she said.

Mary came up beside her. "It's the boys!" She scanned the group knotted on the Marsdens' front lawn. She spotted Tommy, Matt, and Christopher, but she couldn't see Greg. She glanced down the street. Another band was trooping towards the house: the girls! "Practically the whole class is down there!" she exclaimed.

Susie tugged at the window. "I bet they've been looking all over for you, Mary."

Susie was nice to say that, but she couldn't possibly believe it. "They came to see *you*, Susie," Mary said. "Not *me*."

Susie managed to get the window open far enough for her to lean out. "Hey, down there!" she called.

Mary crouched down beside her.

Outside, the two groups — boys and girls — had merged into one and were engaged in such animated conversation that they didn't notice Mary or Susie.

"They didn't come to see either of us," Susie said. "They came to see each other!" She began to laugh. The sound rippled up over Mary like a wave.

Mary started to laugh, too.

13

"If you don't come down from there right this minute, Greg Hopkins, I'm going home!" Mary called.

Behind the basketball backboard on his garage roof, Greg peered down at her. "Sometimes you sound just like my mother," he scoffed.

Mary hated for him to say that. And he knew it.

"I'm already late, Greg!" Her mother was probably frantic. Mary had forgotten to phone her from Susie's. Yet, she couldn't have gone directly home without stopping at Greg's. She needed to talk to him.

Greg stepped around the backboard, spread his arms, and balanced on one foot. "Crane in mud," he said identifying the *t'ai chi* position.

The first time Mary had ever seen him, he was perched on the roof exactly as he was now. Even though she knew now how well-coordinated he was, watching him made her no less queasy today than it had when she'd first seen him.

She turned her back on him. "I'm going," she said and began the march up the Hopkins' long drive. "You can stay up there all night for all I care."

Greg stepped around the board, slid to the edge of the low roof, and jumped to the ground. "What's the rush?" he asked, as he caught up with her.

"I haven't been home yet," Mary told him.

"So?"

"So I always go right home after school."

"That's your first mistake," Greg said. "If you *always* do something, parents get to expect it. You should keep them guessing. It gives them something to do."

"It's different with you," Mary said. "Your parents both work; neither one is home after school. My mother *is*."

Greg chuckled. "It's not your mother, Mags. It's you."

This was not the first time she had heard that. Greg said she depended too much on schedules. He thought she should be more flexible. "Go with the flow," he said often — a quote from his *t'ai chi* teacher. But she was not a spur of the moment person.

Deliberately changing the subject, she asked him, "So where'd *you* go after school?"

He launched into the windmill exercise, twisting at the waist, his arms rotating in opposite directions. "Nowhere."

She stepped back to avoid his flailing arms. "The rest of the boys came over to Susie's."

He stopped midcircle, one arm forward, one back. "How'd you know?"

"I was there."

"You?" His arms fell to his sides. "Were at Susie's?"

Mary nodded. "She asked me over." She shrugged. "So I went."

"I thought you didn't like her."

"*You* said that. I didn't," Mary said. "Why weren't you with the boys?"

"I didn't feel like going to Susie's."

"I thought you liked her."

He grinned. "You said that. I didn't."

"Well, you sure act like you like her."

"She's all right," he said. "Cute and all that, but not worth all the . . . " Unable to find the right word, he shrugged.

"Amy thinks she's boy crazy."

"She has a funny way of showing it," Greg said. "Like today. She just disappeared. There everybody was fighting over her, and she wasn't even there!" He chuckled. "I was the only one who saw her leave."

"What'd they say when you told them she was gone?"

"Me? I didn't tell them. Why should I tell them and spoil all the fun?"

They both laughed.

Growing suddenly serious, Greg asked, "Mary, if you could pick someone from the class — someone to be your . . . boyfriend — who would it be?"

Despite his serious expression, Mary thought he was joking. "No one!" she said emphatically.

"What about . . . Tommy?" he persisted.

Mary rolled her eyes skyward as if to say, Save me!

"Matt?"

Mary groaned.

"Chris?"

She said "Greg!" hoping to put an end to this ridiculous conversation.

A smile broke across his face. "Me? Really?"

"You? My boyfriend?" She giggled. "That's the funniest thing I ever heard!" She broke into a hardy laugh, expecting Greg to join in.

But he didn't!

Mary went to her room immediately after supper. She glanced around at the pale peach walls, the hearts-and-flowers wallpaper border, the patchwork quilt on her bed. She liked the peaceful order of the room. It quieted her mind and helped her organize her thoughts. And they certainly needed organizing today!

Folding a leg under her, she sat at her maple desk, turned on her gooseneck lamp, and opened her math book. But she couldn't concentrate. She kept thinking of her conversation with Greg, wondering why he had asked her whom she would choose to be her boyfriend. He knew her well enough to know it wasn't a subject that interested her. Boys were all right but, except for Greg, she thought it better to have as little to do with them as possible. They weren't . . . serious people. Even Tommy, who was very bright, made fun of school. Sports were all any of them cared about, which made no sense to Mary at all since, aside from their value as exercise, sports were meant to be a diversion, something to take a person's mind off the really important things in life.

She sighed, wishing she had someone to talk to about the changes in the sixth grade. But they were all a part of what was happening, and they wouldn't understand. *She* didn't understand it.

Amy, who rarely called Mary, phoned at seven.

"How come you went to Susie's?" she asked, her tone accusing.

"Because she asked me," Mary said simply. She wasn't going to let Amy make her mad.

"A lot of people ask me places I don't go," Amy shot back.

Mary didn't respond. If Amy wanted an argument, she'd have to find someone else.

"Besides," Amy went on, "I didn't think you liked her."

"I never said I didn't like her." Silently, Mary added, You're the one calling her names all the time.

"But you acted like you didn't."

"When?"

"During the fire drill for one," Amy snapped.

"That didn't have anything to do with Susie." Mary wanted to add, You just wanted to cause trouble, but that would only make Amy madder. Instead, she said, "Listen, Amy, I can't talk now. I have to finish my math."

Amy hung up without saying good-bye.

Almost immediately the phone rang again. Laurie.

Mary could hear voices in the background.

"Hi, Mags," Laurie said. "How are you?"

Mary heard a muffled giggle.

They're all together, Mary thought. She imagined the girls gathered around someone's phone — probably Amy's — having a laugh at her expense. Well, she wouldn't give them the satisfaction of thinking it bothered her. She said, "I'm fine. How about you?"

"Oh, I'm okay. I just thought I'd call, you know, to talk."

"About what?" Mary asked.

"Oh, I don't know. Whatever." There was a long pause during which Mary could hear whispered prompting. "I was wondering," Laurie said finally, "how'd you like Susie's house?"

"Pretty much like any other house," Mary responded.

"Did she say anything?"

"About what?"

"I don't know — anything. Like, about any of the . . . boys or anything."

"No," Mary said.

Someone whispered, "Hang up, Laurie," to which Laurie replied, "No!" Then she said to Mary, "No? Really? What did you talk about?"

"We didn't talk much," Mary answered, waiting with delicious anticipation for the next question.

"What *did* you do?"

"Ate candy," Mary said, emphasizing each word carefully, "the most delicious candy I have ever tasted." Then, she hung up.

The phone rang again. Mary picked it up, said, "I have better things to do than talk to you," and hung up. Although she hated arguments, she felt a satisfying surge of victory.

The next time the phone rang, she waited five rings before she picked it up. She held it to her ear without saying a word.

"Mags?" It was Nina. "Listen, I don't blame you for hanging up on me."

Mary listened for background sounds, but she heard none.

"I mean, what I did at lunch!" Nina went on. "Amy was terrible to you, and all I could think about was Tommy. And yesterday, we had plans, and I just went off to Susie's with everybody else. I did call you and all, but . . . " She paused. "Mags? Are you there?" She paused again. "I just wanted you to know I feel real bad about all that, and — "

Mary couldn't stand to hear the sadness in her friend's voice. "It's okay," she interrupted. "I'm not mad."

"Really?" Nina said. "Let's do something tomorrow, okay?"

"Okay," Mary agreed, adding lightly, "you need all the friends you can get. I mean anyone who flips over Tommy Brennan of all people!"

Nina laughed. "Isn't it weird? I don't even *like* him!"

"Everything's weird," Mary said.

"That's for sure," Nina agreed.

"*Greg* even asked who *I'd* pick for a boyfriend!" Where that had struck her as disturbing before, it seemed hilarious now. She began to laugh, thinking Nina, too, would see the humor in it.

But Nina's voice was serious when she asked, "Who *would* you pick, Mary?"

14

"Were you serious when you asked me about boyfriends?" Mary asked Greg on the way to school. She had thought a lot about that conversation and the one with Nina. Everyone else seemed suddenly interested in this boyfriend/girlfriend thing; maybe Greg, too, had actually caught the fever. If so, she wanted to know.

There was a long pause during which Greg eyed her warily. Finally, he asked, "Why?"

"I think I should know, that's all. I mean we're friends and friends let one another know when . . . they . . . change about things."

A light went on in his dark eyes. "That's exactly why I asked you about it," he said. "I figured maybe you'd picked someone out, and you didn't think you could tell me."

"Why would I think I couldn't tell you?"

He shrugged. "It happens," he said. There was

a wise certainty in his tone as though he spoke from experience. "Liking someone of the opposite sex changes things."

Mary thought she knew exactly what he meant. Nina's crush on Tommy had affected their friendship. Sure, Nina had apologized for her insensitive behavior, but before Tommy, there would've been no need for apology. "You have nothing to worry about," Mary assured him. "I am not about to pick anybody. There is no way I want a *boy*friend. And I *know* you're not going to be silly enough to get a crush on some *girl*."

Greg didn't respond. Instead, he extended an arm and ran the other palm along it from shoulder to fingertip, reversing arms while he took long steps backwards.

Mary knew that move. It was called Repulse Monkey. She stopped and, sighing, turned to watch him. "Gr-*eg*," she said as the gap between them widened. "How can we talk when you're doing *that*?"

He didn't seem to hear her.

She glanced at her Swatch watch. "We're going to be late," she called over her shoulder, speeding up.

He caught up with her. "You worry too much," he said.

"It makes me nervous being late."

He laughed. "How can it? You've never *been* late!"

The playground looked different. Usually, the boys huddled together near the chain-link fence while the girls congregated on the sidewalk near the door. Today, the groups had disbanded into loose clusters of both boys and girls.

Tommy lounged against the fence under the adoring eyes of Amy and Laurie. Jennifer, Marisa, Christopher, and Matt sat on the front stairs, talking and laughing. Everywhere, the scene was the same.

Things might have changed in the sixth grade, but Mary had never expected them to go this far!

"What *is* going on?" she said as she and Greg crossed the street.

"The guys think if they talk to the girls they'll look popular," Greg responded.

"Why would they want to do that?"

"So Susie'll notice them."

Glancing around, Mary said, "But Susie isn't even here!"

Nina ran up beside them. She smiled at Greg. "Hi," she said. "Is that a new jacket?"

Greg glanced down at the hand-me-down jeans jacket he had worn every day for the past month. "No," he said, a mystified note in his voice.

Nina giggled. "I guess I never noticed it before," she said. "It sure looks good on you."

Greg rolled his eyes and backed off towards a couple of the boys who were standing alone together far from any of the girls.

Beaming, Nina waved to him. "Bye, Greg. See you later." Without taking her eyes off him, she said to Mary, "He is so *cute!*" and giggled again.

"Greg?" Mary responded. She had never before thought of him in those terms. To her he was just plain Greg, her best friend. She had never given his looks a second thought. She glanced at him over her shoulder. He caught her eye and smiled. He had a nice smile, she had to admit, and even features. His dark eyes were large and expressive. He had nice hands, too, and *t'ai chi* had taught him to use them gracefully.

When Danny Doucette, a tall, gawky classmate, who was standing beside Greg, smiled and waved at her shyly, she realized she was staring. Blushing, she turned back to Nina. "I suppose he's all right," she conceded.

"All right? He's positively handsome!" Nina exclaimed.

Mary shifted from one foot to the other. For some reason, this conversation was making her very uncomfortable. "I thought you liked Tommy," she said.

Nina waved that away. "I didn't *like* him, Mary.

I've never *liked* him. Picking a boyfriend has nothing to do with *liking*."

"Oh," Mary said. "I thought it did."

"Besides," Nina went on, "you know what he did yesterday at Sweet 'n' Ice? After Susie's, everybody went there, and Tommy held the door for Amy — of all people! — *and* Jennifer. Can you believe that? And he smiled at them just exactly the same way he smiled at me!"

Mary didn't know what that proved. "Maybe he's just getting some manners finally," she said.

Nina glanced back at Greg, saying, "Would you be mad, Mary?"

Mary's forehead creased with the effort of understanding. "If Tommy held the door for Amy and Jennifer?"

Nina laughed. "Oh, Mary," she said. "Sometimes, you are so *fun*ny. I'm not talking about *that*. I'm talking about . . ." She pointed toward Greg, covering her extended finger with her other hand.

Mary's forehead relaxed. "Would I be mad if Greg held the door for Amy and Jennifer? No. It wouldn't bother me at all."

Nina laughed harder.

Ignoring her, Mary continued, "Actually, I'd think it was very nice."

Nina doubled over. "No, no," she sputtered. "I

mean Greg and me! Would you be mad if — "

"Oh," Mary interrupted. "Now I get it." Nina was asking her permission to choose Greg for a boyfriend. Everyone made it sound so simple: A person just decided they wanted another person to be their boyfriend or girlfriend, and it happened. Mary knew better. Greg wasn't interested in having a girlfriend. Hadn't he said as much on the way to school? And even if, by some remote chance, he lost his mind like everyone else had, what difference would it make? Certainly it wouldn't affect their friendship. They wouldn't let it.

"No," she said. "I wouldn't mind. Why should I mind?" She meant that sincerely. Still, her ears burned as if she had just told a big, fat lie. She reached up and pulled her hair down over them.

15

"My how nice everyone looks this morning," Mrs. Anson said.

Today, some of the boys were wearing shirts with collars, and even Amy was wearing a dress.

Mary slid down in her chair. She was the only girl in jeans.

Mrs. Anson smiled at Susie. "I think you've started a trend," she said.

That's for sure, Mary thought. And clothes were only a small part of it.

Nina spent the morning with her head in her hands staring at Greg's profile. Mary could see how uncomfortable it made him. He squirmed in his seat, shot Nina exasperated looks, covered the side of his face with an open hand, and finally turned the back of his head to her. Once, Mrs. Anson asked him if he'd had jumping beans for breakfast, which made everyone, except Greg and Mary, laugh.

The entire class was unusually fidgety all morning. They were up and down like jack-in-the-boxes, running to the pencil sharpener, offering to collect papers, hand them out — anything to allow them to pass by one another's desks where they dropped notes or exchanged playful pokes or grinned at one another in the same sappy way.

At first, both boys and girls would glance at Susie to check her reaction to the proceedings, but when she paid no attention, they seemed to forget all about her.

Mary's stern, unapproving face kept anybody from bothering her. Danny Doucette did approach her desk once with what looked like a note. He hesitated beside her briefly, his face growing redder, and then moved on. By lunchtime, only Mary and Susie seemed exempt from the madness that had gripped the sixth grade.

When the bell rang, Mrs. Anson said, "I have never in my life seen such wiggle worms. I strongly suggest you avoid sugar at lunch." She believed that sugar was at the root of the world's problems. Sugar and jeans.

The class exploded out of the room despite Mrs. Anson's warning to be quiet in the halls. Unnoticed, Mary slipped into the girls' room. Susie came in at her heels.

"Hi," she said, holding up a brown bag. "I

brought my lunch today. I thought maybe we could eat together."

"Oh, sure," Mary said. She tried to imagine how the other girls would take this new development. With Susie at their table, they wouldn't be able to talk about her.

"I couldn't concentrate at all this morning," Susie said on the way out the door.

Who could? Mary thought.

"This class is real different," Susie went on. "Much more . . . social or something. In my other school, the boys and girls didn't pay so much attention to each other."

Mary looked at her in disbelief. While she realized that Susie hadn't been a Merredith Heights sixth-grader long enough to realize how complete a change had come over the class, she found it hard to believe that the girl was completely unaware of her part in the transformation. "They weren't always like this," she said, studying Susie for some indication that she knew more than she was letting on. "Actually, they just got this way."

Susie blinked innocently. "You mean, like, overnight?"

Mary shrugged. "Just about."

Susie's eyes widened. "Gee, Mary," she said, "it sounds like some kind of horror movie or something where everybody goes to bed one way and gets up another." She laughed nervously at the thought.

Mary saw enough truth in that comparison to keep her from joining in.

As Mary and Susie approached the girls' table, Amy and Laurie began moving chairs frantically.

Amy squeezed a chair into the small space between her and Jennifer. "Sit here, Susie," she said. It was more like a command than an invitation.

On the other side of the table, Laurie said, "There's more room here."

Smiling at them both, Susie pulled a vacant chair from the aisle to the end of the table. Mary sat down at the corner beside her.

Immediately, Tommy yanked his chair over and plunked down beside Susie.

Leaning close to her, he said, "How's it going?"

Susie shot Mary a sidelong glance. Her fearful expression seemed to say: Help! I'm in the clutches of a monster!

Mary smiled back.

Amy spotted the exchange. "What's going on?" she demanded.

"Oh, nothing," Susie said, "just a little private joke. Right, Mary?"

"Right," Mary answered. Glancing around the table, she added, "Just a little *private* joke." She noted with satisfaction that she could almost see the steam rising from the tops of the girls' heads.

Tommy got to his feet.

Judging by his expression, Mary knew he thought the joke was on him.

"See ya," he said and drifted back to the boys' table.

Watching after him sadly, Marisa said, "Now look what you did, Mags."

"What did I do?" Mary asked.

"Chased Tommy away," Marisa answered.

"He didn't come over to talk to *you*, Marisa," Amy said.

Marisa shrugged. "So what? He came over, didn't he?"

Amy looked puzzled.

"If *he* came over, maybe some of the other boys might've come over, too," Marisa explained.

"Oh. Right," Amy said. Then she gave Mary a dirty look.

Susie opened her lunchbag.

"Any candy in there?" Laurie asked.

"No," Susie said. "Just some fruit." She extracted a pear and a banana.

Laurie looked down at the sandwich — her second one — in her hand: peanut butter, mayonnaise, and cheese on white bread. She looked at Susie. "Is that *all* you eat?"

"For lunch? Usually," Susie said.

Laurie slipped the sandwich back into her brown bag.

Egged on by the other boys, Richard ambled over holding two open milk cartons. "Put your hands on the table," he told Susie.

Susie glanced up at him, her eyes wide. "Why?"

"I wanna show you something," Richard said.

Susie hesitated.

"Don't do it, Susie," Amy said.

That seemed to be all Susie needed. "Okay," she said.

"Palms down," Richard said.

Susie followed instructions. "Now what?"

"This." Richard placed a carton on the back of each of her hands. "Okay. Now what you do is try to move the cartons off your hands without spilling any milk."

Everyone held their breath as Susie surveyed the situation.

She smiled. "You mean like this?" She leaned forward and removed a carton with her teeth. With the freed hand, she took the carton from her mouth and handed it to Richard. Then she removed the second container and gave that to him.

The girls clapped.

The boys cheered.

Richard's face melted downward. His eyes still

on Susie, he reached toward the table. He set one carton close to the edge — too close! It rocked. He grabbed for it. The side of his hand grazed the other. Both cartons overturned, splashing milk all over him.

Everyone laughed.

Except Susie. She popped up out of her chair to help Richard mop himself off.

Mary caught Greg's eye. The look of admiration in it was unmistakable.

16

A few days later, Nina dropped a folded piece of paper on Mary's desk on the way to the pencil sharpener. On the outside it said: *Don't show this to anyone!!!* Mary made sure she wasn't in Mrs. Anson's line of sight before she opened the note.

> *Roses are red*
> *Vielets are blue.*
> *It makes me happy*
> *Just looking at you.*

A heart-shaped line of circles and *x*'s framed the verse. At the bottom of the page it read: *Don't show this to anyone under pain of death!* Beneath those words was a crude drawing of a skull and crossbones.

Mary glanced up. Nina was still sharpening pencils. She re-read the note. *Vielets?* she repeated to herself. She studied the handwriting. If the words had been written in cursive, she might have been able to identify the author, but they had been printed — something no one in the class had done since third grade. She ripped a piece of paper from her spiral notebook and wrote *Who sent you this?* with a red pen. She placed it at the edge of her desk facing toward the aisle so that Nina would see it on her way back to her place. Now, she would put the verse on top of her own note where Nina could just slip it off her desk.

Nina's note was gone!

Mary lifted her notebook to look underneath. Not there. She shook the book thinking the note might be inside. It wasn't. Maybe she had accidentally knocked it to the floor when she got out the piece of paper. She looked down to her left. No note. Down to her right. Nothing.

Nina had finished sharpening her pencils.

Mary swiveled to look at the desk behind her. Laurie gave her a poke. She raised herself on her elbows to look over Christopher Carey's shoulder.

Mrs. Anson's eyes shot up above her glasses. "Mary Agnes?" she said.

Unhooking the hair from behind her right ear, Mary popped out of her seat. "Yes, Mrs. Anson?"

"Is there anything you need?"

"No, thank you, Mrs. Anson." She sat down.

When Mrs. Anson returned her attention to correcting papers, Greg, who was sitting sideways in his chair, leaned across the aisle. "This what you're looking for?" he whispered and slid Nina's folded note across her desk.

Nina started down the aisle. She paused beside Mary's desk, read her friend's written question, rolled her eyes toward Greg and shrugged. She thought Greg might have sent her the verse, but she wasn't certain. She slipped the folded note off the desk into her cupped palm.

At that exact moment, Mrs. Anson glanced up again. "What *is* the problem there?" she asked, her eyes focused on Mary.

Mary bounced out of her chair so quickly she knocked her spiral notebook to the floor and Nina into Greg's lap.

The class roared.

Mrs. Anson gave them a narrow-eyed warning look. Then she repeated her question.

As Nina struggled to her feet, Mary searched her mind for something to say. Her instinct was to tell the truth, but she couldn't do that. If she did, Mrs. Anson would ask to see Nina's note, and she would probably read it to the entire class. Nina would never speak to her again. She opened her mouth, hoping there were words in it.

"I was just borrowing some paper," Nina piped up. She reached around Mary and snatched the spiral sheet from her desk, holding it up as proof.

Mrs. Anson squinted at the paper. Even from that distance she could see the red writing. Now she would ask to see the paper. Then she would ask what Mary's scribbled question meant and Nina would have to show her the verse.

Mary held her breath waiting.

Finally, Mrs. Anson said, "If I were you, Nina, I'd borrow a *clean* sheet."

Everything was out of focus for the remainder of the afternoon — except Nina's note. It kept popping into Mary's head. She doubted that Greg had written it. It wasn't like him not to sign something he had written. He took great pride in his signature and had been known to sign papers that weren't even his. He couldn't have a crush on Nina. If he did, he wouldn't act so uncomfortable with her attentions. Nina's wishful thinking, that's all it was.

Mary glanced across the aisle. When Greg responded, as he always did, with a smile, she would know she was right.

His head on his fists and his eyes downcast, he was reading the assigned short story. He did not look up.

Mary cleared her throat.

Still, Greg ignored her.

She stared holes in him. He never moved.

He *had* written that stupid note! No wonder he wouldn't look at her: He was too embarrassed. She turned her back on him.

"Pssst, Mags," he hissed.

She looked over her shoulder.

He pointed to the story and turned his thumbs down.

He wasn't even thinking about Nina! He hadn't written that note. He couldn't have written that note.

She smiled. She wouldn't even mention it to him. She'd been ridiculous to imagine — even for a moment — that Greg was the author of such a stupid verse.

The bell rang.

She leaned across the aisle. "Greg, how do you spell *violets*?"

"V-i-e-l-e-t-s," he said without hesitation.

Mary catapulted from her chair. "How could you *do* such a thing?" she snapped.

Greg shrunk in his seat. "E-i?" he asked sheepishly.

Mary stomped out of the room. Someone called out her name, but she kept moving toward the girls' room where she thought she'd be left alone.

Once inside, she stared at her image in the mirror. She saw red: red ears, red face, red neck.

This is ridiculous, she told herself. So what if

Greg had written Nina that stupid verse. It didn't mean they couldn't be friends. The important question was *why* had he written it? Did he really like Nina? Or . . . had he merely caved in to the pressures in the class? If so, he wasn't worth having as a friend!

The door flew open and the girls burst in, all talking at once. The words swirled around Mary like broken branches in rushing water.

"Mine is — "

" — all the same!"

"Who wrote — ?!"

Mary's head hurt with the effort of trying to the grab onto something solid.

Finally, Amy's voice rose above the others. "Mine is the original," she said brandishing a piece of paper. "You all got xerox copies."

"How can you tell?" Nina asked. "They all look exactly alike."

Everyone held pieces of paper against Amy's sheet.

"They wouldn't be *exactly* alike unless he used an original to make copies," she said, a patronizing edge to her voice. "I got the original."

In the clamor that followed Amy's conclusion, the storm in Mary's mind quieted. She glanced from one to the other: Jennifer, Laurie, Marisa,

Amy, Nina. Greg had sent each of them the same note!

Feeling numb, she started out of the room.

"Mags, wait!" Nina called. "We're all going to Sweet 'n' Ice. The boys, too."

At the door, Mary froze. She and Nina had plans for this afternoon. Once again, Nina had forgotten. "Have a good time," she said and left the room.

She passed by Danny Doucette on the way out of school.

"Hi, Mary," he said, smiling broadly.

She didn't answer.

She hurried along the broad concrete walk, past the flagpole, across the street, down the block. Suddenly, she stopped.

Ahead, Greg was walking Mrs. Popek's wall. With Susie Marsden!

17

At home, Mrs. Gardner was on the phone. "Here she is now, Greg," she said and handed Mary the receiver.

Instantly, Mary's breathing turned ragged. How could she talk to Greg now? She was too upset. She covered the mouthpiece while she took several deep breaths. Finally she put the phone to her ear. "Hi," she said, trying to sound nonchalant. "I just got home."

"I had to call you," Greg went on. "I got an idea for the science fair."

His calm, easy manner infuriated Mary. How could he act as though nothing had happened?

"You know how Mrs. Anson said the best ideas were right under our noses?" he said. "Well, what d'ya think about *t'ai chi?*"

"*T'ai chi?*" Mary wondered what that had to do with science.

"I figured I'd do a study on how it affects people.

Like if they do the exercises before a test? Do they get a better grade? Or when they're mad — stuff like that. See if it really calms a person." He paused. "What d'ya think?"

Despite her anger, Mary got caught up in the idea. "It sounds great!" she said. "And nobody else'll do it. How'd you ever think of it?"

"I was talking to Susie after school, and I showed her some *t'ai chi* moves and she said, 'That'd be great for the project.' "

"Susie gave you the idea?" Mary couldn't keep the surprise from her voice.

"Like I said, she's pretty smart. And I take back what I said about her not being able to spell. She even taught me how to spell *violets*."

Anger welled up inside Mary. "Too bad you didn't know how to spell it before you wrote all those notes," she said, and hung up on him.

Greg wasn't at the corner in the morning. Mary waited awhile hoping he'd show up. She needed to talk to him. She felt terrible about yesterday. Whenever they'd had a disagreement in the past — a rare occurrence — they had talked it out. This time was different. She should have come right out and asked him what was going on. She would do that this morning if he ever showed up. Maybe he had decided to stay home. She had been tempted to do that herself. And she hadn't missed a day since the third grade.

Finally, she swung by his house; he wasn't there either.

She took her time walking towards school. It wouldn't have mattered to her if she were late. It wouldn't matter if she got there at all. That's what all this boy-girl nonsense was doing to her.

Susie hopped out of her father's van and joined Mary two blocks from school. "Where's Greg?" she asked.

"I don't know," Mary said. She cast a wary glance toward Susie. "Why?"

"No reason," Susie said. "He usually walks with you, that's all."

Except when he walks with you, Mary thought, but she said, "He's getting as weird as everybody else."

Susie nodded. "It's all this boy-girl stuff. It always changes everything."

Mary shook her head. "I don't understand any of this," she said more to herself than to Susie.

Standing alone near the crosswalk in front of school, Danny Doucette waved as the girls approached.

Mary assumed he was waiting for Susie. Good,

she thought. With Susie occupied with him, she could slip away and find a quiet place to think.

"Hi," Danny said as the girls crossed the street. Looking directly at Mary, he said, "Can I — uh — talk to you a minute?"

Mary didn't notice. She was too busy scanning the playground. Greg and Nina stood talking near the front door. He must've left home early so he could meet her. Maybe he had even walked Nina to school while Mary was standing alone on the corner, waiting for him.

She looked away. Sixth-graders were scattered all over the place — mostly in twos! Amy and Tommy by the fence; Laurie and Matt next to the water fountain; it looked as if only Jennifer stood alone.

Susie poked her. "Mary?"

Jennifer moved to one side. She wasn't alone! Christopher Carey was there, looking up at her devotedly.

The shortest person in the class and the tallest person. It seemed absurd. In spite of herself, Mary giggled.

"Mary," Susie said, "Danny wants to know if . . ."

Watching Jennifer and Christopher, Mary said, "It's okay. You can talk to him. I don't mind."

"But I — uh — " Danny sputtered.

Susie came to his rescue with, "He doesn't want to talk to *me*, Mary. He wants to talk to *you*."

Mary's attention snapped back. She looked at Danny. "Me? You want to talk to *me*?"

Danny blushed. "I — uh — "

Saying, "See ya," Susie darted away.

"What about?" Mary asked Danny.

Danny took a deep audible breath. "I — uh — was — uh — wondering," he said and then stopped to shift from one foot to the other.

"You were wondering what?" Mary urged him. If he didn't hurry and say whatever it was he had to say, the bell would ring.

Danny cleared his throat. "Wouldyougowithme" — he spoke quickly, spitting out the words as if they were all strung together — "somewhere-afterschool?"

Mary stared at him. Up until two days ago, Danny had hardly spoken to her. And now all of a sudden — What *was* he talking about? Where could he possibly want her to go? It must have something to do with school. "Do you need help with homework or something?"

He ran his tongue along his thin lips. "For a yogurt or an ice cream," he managed at last.

Mary cocked her head to one side. "Why?"

He shrugged. "I just thought," he shrugged

again, "it'd be . . . fun. You and me." He edged away. "But you're probably busy today."

As he spoke, realization dropped inside her word by word like an icicle. He was asking her for a date! Panicked, she shrieked, "Are you asking me for a *date*?!"

Danny's face went white. He turned on his heel and dashed off just as the bell rang.

Although she tried all morning, Mary could not keep her mind off Danny Doucette. Nor her eyes. They kept sliding in his direction. And every time she looked at him, he cast a grinning sidelong glance at her.

When Mrs. Anson called on her during reading, she couldn't find the place. When she went to pass out the spelling papers, she dropped them all over the floor.

Laurie poked her during social studies.

Startled, Mary swiveled around.

Laurie held up a notebook sheet on which she had drawn a big red heart encircling the initials *M.G. + D.D.*

"Give me that," Mary hissed. She grabbed for the paper, but Mrs. Anson, who had come silently down the aisle, beat her to it.

Mary slid down in her chair and squeezed her eyes closed. Holding her breath, she waited for her teacher to show that awful, lopsided heart to the entire class.

Slowly, rhythmically, Mrs. Anson's heels clicked, along the floor toward the front of the room.

Mary opened one eye.

Mrs. Anson turned to face the class, holding the sheet of paper in both hands as though she were about to read it.

Mary shut her eye.

"I'd say this entire class has a touch of spring fever," their teacher said, "except it isn't even spring." There was a lilt in the last few words almost as though Mrs. Anson were singing them.

Mary heard a ripping sound. Her eyes flew open. She scooched to the edge of her chair and leaned out slightly into the aisle. Mrs. Anson was tearing the paper to shreds and dropping it into the wastebasket.

Which is what Mary wanted to do with the last two weeks!

18

When the lunch bell rang, Greg leaned toward Mary. "So," he said. "You and Danny?"

Mary could feel herself blushing. "Capital *n*, capital *o*," she said.

Greg raised an eyebrow. "I don't know," he said. "It looks . . . serious."

Mary stood up. "Yeah, well, things aren't always the way they look, Greg."

A lopsided grin spread across his face. "You got that right," he said.

She felt he was trying to tell her something that had nothing to do with Danny Doucette. "What's *that* supposed to mean?" she asked.

He just kept grinning at her.

She turned on her heel and left the room.

In the gym, the girls were poring over the makeup ads in *Seventeen*.

When Mary sat down, Laurie said, "I saw Mags

flirting with Danny," and Amy added, "We *all* saw Mags flirting with Danny."

"I was not flirting with Danny," Mary snapped. She turned to Nina, "Was I flirting with Danny?"

Nina wasn't paying attention. She was drawing tiny hearts on her fingernails with a red marker. In each, she inserted a different boy's initials.

"I was not flirting with Danny," Mary repeated emphatically.

Danny passed by the table sideways. "Hi, Mary," he said, grinning shyly.

A scowl on her face, Mary barked, "Hi."

"Mags likes Danny," Laurie said, and everyone at the table took up the chant.

"Mary Agnes Doucette," Nina said dreamily. After a pause, she added, "It doesn't sound right."

"Her initials'd be *M-A-D*," Marisa said. "We could call her *Mad*."

Nina chuckled. "We could call her *that* already," she teased.

Mary pushed herself away from the table. "I think I'm going to be sick," she said.

"That's because you haven't eaten," Jennifer said.

"Love does that to a person," Marisa put in. "They lose their appetite."

Laurie's eyes lit up. "Really?"

"This is all so stupid," Mary said.

Amy guffawed. "If you think it's so *stupid*, Mags, then why are you flirting with Danny?" She looked around the table smugly.

"I already told you," Mary protested. "I am not flirting with Danny Doucette."

"Why not?" Laurie asked. "What's wrong with him?"

Mary groaned. "Nothing's *wrong* with him."

"Do you like somebody else better?" Laurie persisted.

"Greg," Nina answered for her. "Mags likes Greg the best."

"I do not like Greg!" Mary exploded.

Everybody stared at her incredulously.

Mary pulled her hair over her ears. "I mean I *like* Greg — of course I like Greg — but I don't like him the way you mean."

"He likes *you*," Nina told her. "He told me he did. That's why he wouldn't be my boyfriend."

A rush of emotion made Mary's heart pound. She didn't want Greg as a boyfriend. It would spoil everything. And all this talk about it was unsettling. She shot to her feet. "Greg does not like me!"

No one paid any attention to her vehement denial. Instead, they began to talk among themselves as though she weren't standing right there.

"If Greg's her boyfriend," Amy said, "then I don't think she should flirt with Danny."

"Right," Jennifer agreed. "It isn't fair."

"No one should have *two* boyfriends," Laurie added.

"I don't have *any* boyfriends!" Mary said, a frustrated edge to her voice. "And I don't want any either!" She whirled around and bumped into Matt.

He stood near the table, his thumbs hooked through his belt loops. "Hi, girls," he said. "You fighting over me?"

"Very funny!" Amy said.

"How'd you like the little verse you got yesterday?" he asked.

There was a stunned silence.

Mary's stomach tightened. Matt had written the verse! She should have known. He was a worse speller than Greg.

The girls exchanged glances. Then, as if on cue, they got up and moved toward Matt, hurling angry words at him. He put up his arms protectively as though to ward off stones.

Mary dashed out of the room. She had been wrong to assume Greg had written the note. Wrong not to have talked to him about her suspicions. She had to find him.

Outside, she saw Greg at the far corner of the basketball court. Susie was with him, but Mary was so intent on seeing Greg, she barely noticed. "Greg!" she called.

He and Susie were doing *t'ai chi* exercises, and he didn't look up.

Mary raced toward him. She had to talk to him before the bell rang. Breathless, she ran up beside him. "Greg, I have to talk to you!"

"Can't now," he said. "I'm doing an experiment — seeing how *t'ai chi* exercises affect Susie."

"Hi, Mary," Susie said, smiling sweetly.

Ignoring her, Mary said, "Grr-*egg*! It's important!"

"So's this," he said and turned toward Susie. He shifted his weight to his left foot, placed the right one forward on a slight angle with the heel raised. "Cat stance," he said, but Susie wasn't watching.

She was looking at Mary, concern in her eyes. "What's wrong, Mary?" she asked.

"You should know!" Mary snapped. "It's all your fault!"

Susie took a step backwards as though she'd been hit. Her stunned expression made Mary feel awful, but she continued to lash out. "Well, it is," she said. "Before you came here, everything was fine. We were all friends and school was fun and now all anybody thinks about is boyfriends and girlfriends and nobody is the same anymore and I hate it!"

"Susie," Greg said urgently. "Take deep breaths! Relax!"

Susie's chest heaved.

"That's it!" Greg said. "Breathe! In! Out!"

Mary had never attacked anyone this way before. It made her feel as though she were growing smaller and smaller. If she uttered another word, she would surely disappear. Yet the sight of Susie standing there, breathing deeply, and the sound of Greg's enthusiastic prompting made her so angry she couldn't keep herself from saying, "And I hate you, too!"

Susie inhaled deeply. And stopped breathing. Her mouth was open and her eyes wide. Finally, her gaze unflinching, she let out a long, slow breath.

Mary turned and stumbled away.

Behind her, Greg said, "It works, Susie! *T'ai chi* really works!"

19

Mary had knots in her stomach all afternoon. She kept sliding her gaze toward Susie, wondering how she felt. Susie didn't seem any different. She paid attention to class work, and answered sweetly when she was called on to recite. She even seemed to read better than she had that first day. There were no indications that she was smarting from the hurt Mary had inflicted.

Mary, on the other hand, felt wounded. She wished she could relive those few moments with Susie. She should never have said any of those things. If it hadn't been for her anger at the other girls and at Greg, she never would have said them. That was no excuse, she realized. What she had done, she had done. She had no one to blame but herself. And an apology would probably be useless. Susie would never accept it. If she were Susie, she wouldn't easily forgive and forget.

Greg kept trying to catch her eye, but Mary

avoided his glance. She knew it would be disapproving.

When the final bell rang, Susie turned to her.

Mary lowered her eyes and busied herself getting her books together.

"Mary?" Susie said.

Mary's heart pounded. Susie had probably sat there quietly all afternoon gathering her ammunition. Now she was going to let Mary have it.

Avoiding Susie's eyes, Mary said, "I gotta go," and hurried toward the door.

A smiling Danny Doucette appeared out of nowhere.

Mary brushed past him and dashed down the hall. She ran all the way home as though something were chasing her.

At four o'clock when the back doorbell rang, Mary was sitting at the kitchen table, her mother's medical dictionary open before her. She was looking for a disease with a long name and a slow cure. She'd decided never to leave her house again.

She glanced out the window behind her.

Greg stood outside the door in a horse stance, knees bent, arms extended.

Maybe if she didn't answer the door, he'd think she wasn't home and go away.

With a shift of his weight from his heels to the balls of his feet, he was able to push the bell again.

She had to let him in. He was a true friend to come to see her after the way she'd acted. She'd tell him how sorry she was. Maybe he could help her decide what to do about Susie.

She went to the door and opened it.

He straightened slowly and lowered his arms. "Hi," he said. His eyes were wary as though he didn't know what to expect.

"Hi," she responded. "Wanna come in?"

"Why don't you come out?"

Mary looked around the yard. The sun's rays angled through the trees, bright with fall colors. A lone sparrow perched on the telephone wire overhead. A squirrel sat on its haunches at the base of the hickory tree, nibbling a scrap.

"Okay," she agreed and reached for her red cardigan on the hook beside the door. She had all evening to choose a disease and all night to practice the symptoms.

She and Greg immediately fell into step as they ambled down the drive.

"Where're we going?" Mary asked.

Greg shrugged. "Nowhere particular."

That was fine with Mary. They often just took off, walking side by side with no destination in mind. Sometimes, like today, they were quiet.

Other times, they were so full of talk they hardly took notice of their surroundings. Either way, being two friends together was the important part.

Mary was the first to speak. "I suppose you and Susie talked about what happened," she said.

He looked at her briefly, his eyes coolly appraising. "She was real upset about it — about you being mad at her."

She's the one who should be mad, Mary thought.

"The *t'ai chi* helped, though — it really works. My project's going to be great. And I told her not to worry." He grinned. "That you were mad at everybody." The grin faded. "Why're you mad at her?"

"I'm not," Mary said quickly. "I *was*. Sort of," she amended. "I mean, I *thought* I was, but I wasn't."

Greg chuckled. "That's about as clear as mud."

Mary sighed deeply before she launched into the entire story. As she spoke, she felt better, less sad, less guilty, and she began to understand why she had lashed out at Susie.

"I guess it's me I'm really mad at," she concluded, "because I don't know what's happening anymore, and I keep thinking if Susie hadn't come along . . . " Her voice trailed off.

"It's not Susie," Greg assured her.

"I know that." On one level she did know and understand that Susie was not responsible for the change in the sixth grade; on another, she wasn't so sure. "I mean, I guess I know that. You're saying it would've happened anyway."

"Sooner or later," he said.

"Without Susie, it would've been later."

Greg ran his hand along a mulberry bush branch from base to tip, stripping it of leaves.

Mary cringed. Every time she attempted that, she was stuck by a thorn.

"It might've been Susie in the beginning," he said as he showered the air with the tiny green leaves. "Everybody wanted to be her friend. It made them seem more popular or something, but now . . . " he shrugged.

"Now, everyone's gone crazy," Mary completed his thought.

"I think it's kinda . . . neat — what's happening."

"What's neat about it?" Mary pressed. "Look what it's already done to us."

He shot her an inquiring glance.

"About the notes," she explained. "I suspected you right away. Any other time, I would've just come out and asked, but I didn't. And it's because I'm all confused about everything."

Greg thought about that for a long time. Finally he took a deep breath. "I don't know about that — why you didn't come out and ask me. You should've."

"I know," Mary agreed, "that's what I said. When I found out Matt wrote that stupid verse! Why'd he write it anyway?"

Greg shrugged. "He's trying to be as popular as Tommy."

Mary chuckled. "Who says Tommy's popular?"

"Tommy," Greg said. "And Matt believes everything Tommy says."

"This whole thing is getting out of hand," Mary said.

Greg waved that away. "You're taking it all too seriously, Mags."

"I'm not the one taking it seriously," she objected. "It's everybody else!"

"It's nothing to get so uptight about," Greg persisted. "Go with the flow. Things change. If you like somebody — "

"Nina says none of it has anything to do with whether you like a person or not," she interrupted. "She doesn't like Tommy and just because he was nice to her — opened the door for her or some stupid thing — she thought she was" — she held her hands over her heart and rolled her eyes skyward — "in love."

"For a minute or two," Greg joked. "Besides, Tommy doesn't like Nina."

"I know that. That's the whole point. They don't like each other!"

"We like each other," Greg said, giving her a sidelong glance.

"That's because we're friends," Mary said, following her own train of thought. "Before everybody understood that, but now, I don't know. Nina is spreading it all over that you don't just like me, but that you . . . *like* me." She laughed. "I know you said that — *if* you said that — " She squinted at him. "Did you say that?" When he responded with a noncommital murmur, she continued, "I know it was to keep Nina from bothering you, but I didn't like it, Greg. I didn't like it at all."

"Why? You afraid Danny Doucette'll find out?" he asked.

"Danny Doucette!" Mary rolled her eyes. "He never paid the least bit of attention to me before and now he's everywhere! It's making me very nervous."

"Well, if you don't like him, why not me?"

Saying, "Grr-*eggg*," Mary swatted at him with an open hand. "Be serious."

"I am," he said, pausing to look at her. "It might be a good idea — you and me." There was a mis-

chievous twinkle in his eye. "At least it'd keep
Danny Doucette from following you all over."

Mary made a face.

"Be my girlfriend, and he'll leave you alone."
He studied her for a reaction before adding,
"Well? What d'ya think?"

"I think this whole thing is like a disease," she
said, "a contagious disease. And," she added
darkly, to Greg's mystification, "it wasn't the one
I was looking for."

20

Indicating the Sweet 'n' Ice storefront, Greg said, "Just what the doctor ordered." He started for the door.

Mary hesitated. "I didn't bring any money."

"I'll loan you some," Greg offered.

"I don't like borrowing."

"So I'll treat."

Still, Mary hung back. "Everyone's probably in there," she said. She was in no mood to be caught in the flirting frenzy that was undoubtedly in progress just behind the door.

"It's too late. They've probably all gone home." Greg peered inside. "The coast is clear," he assured her as he opened the door to let her enter.

She stepped past him with apprehension. It had been just over two weeks since she'd been here, but it seemed much longer. So much else had changed, she expected this place, too, would be different. She was relieved to find her fears unfounded. Everything from the wineberry-and-rose quartz color scheme to the casual warmth of the place was just as it had always been.

"I'll have a chocolate cyclone," she told the girl behind the counter, "with M & M's on top."

"You always have that," Greg said. "Why don't you try something different?"

"I like it," she explained simply. Today, especially, with everything else in turmoil, she needed the reassurance of being able to do things as she had always done them.

Greg didn't push it. "I'll have a doubleheader," he said, "one peanut butter and one blueberry cheesecake."

Mary made a face. She couldn't imagine a worse combination. "Just what the doctor ordered," she joked.

They ambled toward home, enjoying the cold, smooth sweetness of their yogurt and the comfort of each other's company. The small, cozy houses along the way glowed in the day's last golden sun-rays, and the maple trees dabbed the tidy, fading lawns with dropped spots of riotous color.

Mary felt fortunate to live in such a beautiful place and to have Greg for her best friend.

"I've been thinking," she said. "What if you hadn't moved here? We wouldn't even know each other. Isn't that an awful thought?"

"Don't think it," Greg replied.

She sighed. Without their classmates there jabbering boy-girl talk, she could almost make herself believe that nothing had changed. She cocked her head to look at him. "I'm so glad we didn't run into any of the other kids."

Greg met her eyes. He smiled. "Me, too," he said.

When Mary bounced in through the back door, her mother was in the kitchen. Her face was full of concern. "Are you all right, Mary?" she asked.

Mary was puzzled. "I'm fine. Why?"

Her mother's gaze fell on the open medical dictionary.

"Oh, that," Mary said. "I was just looking up diseases."

Her mother's face relaxed. "Did you find any you liked?" she joked.

Laughing, Mary shook her head. "I couldn't even find one I could pronounce!" she said.

She felt so good that she couldn't even relate to the girl who, just hours before, had decided never to leave the house again. She hadn't been thinking clearly then. Everything was jumbled together in her mind like yarn in a basket, and she couldn't locate the end that would unravel it all. Now, she knew she could sort through her tangled thoughts. Being with Greg had helped her to see that. Friends did that for you. Even if they didn't directly say or do anything to clear up the muddle, being with them helped you to know what you had to do.

The first thing Mary had to do was call Susie to apologize. It would be difficult and the girl might not forgive her, but she had to do it just the same.

Her stomach tightened as she dialed the number. Each ring seemed to reverberate through her, jangling her nerves, making her heart pound. When Susie answered, Mary was as breathless as she would have been if she'd just run a mile.

"Hi, Susie." She paused to take a couple of deep breaths.

"Mary! Hi!" Susie sounded happy to hear from her. "I was just going to call you."

"You were?"

"I'll bet that's why you called me — 'cuz you *knew*."

There she goes again, Mary thought, assuming I know things I couldn't possibly know. "I didn't know," she said. "How would I know?"

"Your *feelings*," Susie said, surprise in her voice.

"Oh, I can't read minds," Mary said.

"I'll bet you could if you tried," Susie responded.

"Why were you going to call me?" Mary asked, deliberately changing the subject.

"Because you're mad at me and I just wanted to say I'm sorry."

Mary couldn't believe what she heard. It was as if someone had switched scripts and Susie was reading the wrong lines. "You didn't do anything, Susie," she said. "I'm the one. I was awful to you. I wouldn't blame you if you never forgave me."

Susie laughed. "That'd be pretty stupid. We're friends, aren't we? Besides, I don't believe in staying mad at anybody. It wears a person out."

Mary agreed with that. She had been angry with nearly everyone in the sixth grade. It hadn't done her a bit of good. Certainly, she couldn't change things back to the way they were. And being upset about it had interfered with her schoolwork and her usual sense of well-being.

What she had to do was go with the flow. Susie knew that, and she didn't even take *t'ai chi*.

21

Mary was so excited about her decision that she didn't notice the chill in the air next morning.

"Greg, I thought about what you said yesterday," she told her friend when they met on the corner, "and I think you're right."

His hands buried in his jacket pockets, Greg looked at her warily. "About what?"

"I think you should be my boyfriend."

Greg's expression transformed to one of delighted surprise. "Well, all right!" he said.

"We'll only be pretending, but — "

Greg nodded. "Pretending. Right."

" — no one else'll know that," Mary concluded. "I think it'll work just like you said, Greg. If you're my boyfriend, then Danny Doucette'll leave me alone. The girls'll stop pestering you, too. Besides that, we'll fit in better."

"Right," Greg said.

"Like you say, 'Go with the flow.' " Mary smiled triumphantly. "Of course we don't have to be as sappy as everyone else — drawing hearts all over everything like they do — but I suppose we do have to . . . act a little different."

Greg grinned at her. "Sometimes you sound just like my mother," he said.

Mary gave him an impatient swat. "This is serious, Greg," she admonished him. "We have to get it all worked out before we get to school. We have to decide how you should act, because boyfriends don't act like ordinary friends."

"Neither do girlfriends," Greg put in.

"That's the problem," Mary said, looking to him for a solution.

He shrugged. "So, you tell me, what should we do?"

"I guess we should call one another a lot," Mary offered.

"And I should walk you to school," Greg suggested.

"And smile a lot — we should smile when we see one another."

"And when we think of each other — we should smile then, too."

"And tell one another things we've never told anybody."

After a brief pause, they turned to look at one

another. "We do all those things now," they said simultaneously.

"So how's anybody gonna know things've changed?" Greg asked.

Mary sighed. "I guess we'll just have to . . . tell them."

They walked the last block in silence. Mary thought about their new status. This boyfriend/girlfriend business might not be so bad after all. If their behavior didn't alter, their friendship would remain intact. And the pretense, a shared secret, might even bring them closer together.

"You know, Greg, this might even be fun," Mary said.

Greg wasn't listening. He was surveying the playground. "Danny's waiting for you again," he told her.

Danny waved and smiled.

"Do something, Greg," Mary instructed as she and Greg crossed the street.

He grabbed her hand. "Smile at me," he said.

She yanked her hand from his. Mrs. Anson would have a fit if she saw them holding hands. Besides, his hand was cold. "I don't feel like smiling."

Mary was face to face with Danny. "Oh, hi, Danny," she said. "I — we didn't see you standing there."

Danny's grin widened. "Hi, Mary," he said.

Greg slid in between them. "So I'll see you after school, Mags?"

Mary didn't know what he was talking about. She had made plans with Susie for after school. She opened her mouth to tell him so, but he rolled his eyes toward Danny. "Oh!" she said remembering she had a role to play. "After school." She smiled. "Right."

Greg edged away. "I can't wait," he said.

Mary thought that sounded sappy, but she went along with it. "Me, neither."

Grinning and waving his fingers at her, Greg backstepped toward a small group of the boys.

He didn't even look like himself! It was that silly smirk. Mary wanted to dash after him and wipe it off his face. Instead, she smiled and waved to him. When her face started to hurt, she turned to Danny.

His own smile had slid off center. He seemed to be frozen.

They stood there silently, facing one another. Danny's face changed color slowly. Judging by the creeping heat she felt, Mary knew hers was turning red, too.

She felt she should say something to Danny — tell him that she and Greg were a couple, but she couldn't find the words.

Finally, Danny said, "You and Greg?"

Averting her eyes, she nodded.

The smile slid off his face entirely. His shoulders drooped. "Oh," he said.

He looked so dejected. Mary wanted to say something funny to cheer him up, but she couldn't think of a single word, funny or otherwise.

Nina came galloping to the rescue. "Hi, Danny," she said, "is that a new jacket?"

Danny glanced down at his dark green windbreaker. He looked at Nina, at Mary, the jacket. Then, he trotted off.

"He is so *cute*," Nina said.

"Maybe you could be his girlfriend," Mary suggested. "Maybe we could all do something together sometime, you and Danny and . . . Greg and me." It was all she could do to keep from blurting out, "We're pretending to be boyfriend and girlfriend."

Nina gaped at her. "You and *Greg*?!"

Mary shrugged as if to say, "You know how it is."

Nina danced in a circle. "I knew it! I knew it all along!"

Susie ran up. "I've got something for you, Mary," she said. She fanned out a deck of cards.

Mary glanced at them absently. They contained various symbols: a cross, circle, square . . . . She had seen cards like these before. "Extrasensory Perception cards," she said, wondering why Susie had brought them to school.

Susie didn't have the chance to explain because, just then, Nina interrupted, "Susie! Did you know that Mags and Greg like each other?"

Nina made it her business to tell everyone about Mary and Greg. Mary was relieved that she didn't have to do it herself. Telling Danny and Nina had been much more difficult than she had anticipated. Lying was against her nature, and even though she told herself it was only a role-playing game, she was uncomfortable with it. She worried that someone would detect the ruse, but no one did. They seemed to think the pairing of her and Greg was inevitable.

Amy summarized the class' attitude when she said, "So what else is new?"

Mary had mixed emotions about the reaction. She was relieved that her classmates accepted the sham without question, making explanations unnecessary. At the same time, she resented their assuming she was so predictable that they knew what she was going to do before she herself knew.

Greg didn't seem to be having similar problems. He accepted his role wholeheartedly. A devoted look on his face, he smiled at Mary all morning.

141

When she entered the room, he smiled. When she left it, he smiled. When she stood to recite, he smiled. When she sat down, he smiled. He smiled when she gave a correct answer and when she was wrong.

It made her so self-conscious that her ears burned. She kept covering them but, still, she could feel them poking, flame-red, through her fine brown hair. She scowled at Greg a couple of times and mouthed, "Stop it!" but he kept right on smiling.

By lunchtime, she was ready to explode, and when Greg suggested they eat together, she stormed off without responding.

"I can't wait till it snows," she said as she joined the other girls at the table.

Everyone focused on her, waiting for an explanation.

Past experience had taught her that boys could not resist packing snow into smooth icy balls and pitching them at the girls. Mary had always dreaded winter for that reason. Now, she'd prefer a direct hit with a snowball to the boys' sappy smiles. "The boys'll start throwing snowballs at us," she explained, "and things'll be back to normal."

The girls exchanged puzzled glances. Then Nina

said, "How do you hold hands in the winter?"

Now it was Mary's turn to look puzzled.

"I was wondering that, too," Jennifer said. "This morning it was so cold. I was wishing I had my mittens and — "

"You shouldn't hold hands when you're wearing *mittens*," Amy said.

"Why not?" Laurie asked.

"Because it wouldn't be like holding hands then; it'd be like holding . . . mittens."

"What about gloves?" Marisa asked.

Amy rolled her eyes. "It's the same *thing*, Marisa."

"But if it's cold, and you take off your mittens or gloves or whatever," Marisa said, "your hands could . . . freeze!"

Nina's eyes went dreamy. "His hand and your hand — frozen together. That is so *romantic*!"

Mary crumbled her lunch bag. This conversation was ridiculous!

"What're you doing after school?" Laurie asked her.

"I'm going to Susie's," Mary said.

"Does Greg want to do that?" Jennifer wanted to know.

"What's Greg got to do with it?" Mary asked.

The girls looked appalled. They all started talking at once. "You mean, he's not going with you?" someone said, and, "Did you ask him if it was okay?"

"I don't have to ask his permission," Mary snapped.

"Matt'd be real jealous if I went somewhere without asking him first," Jennifer said.

"Matt?" Mary repeated. "I thought Christopher was your boyfriend."

"That didn't work out," Amy put in.

"Everybody thought he was my little brother," Jennifer added.

"So who's Christopher's girlfriend?" Mary asked.

"Marisa of course," Amy answered.

Marisa smiled and lowered her eyes demurely.

"Where've you been, Mags?" Laurie asked.

As she sat there listening to the girls talk, Mary asked herself the same question. Apparently, without her having been aware of it, things in the sixth grade had changed once again. This boy-girl business had begun as a kind of game. Everybody had flirted with everybody. The couples that had formed were temporary and changed rapidly. Now, the pairing off was becoming more serious and permanent.

Mary wasn't sure how she and Greg fit into all

this. If pretending to be a couple meant they couldn't have friends, too, then she didn't want any part of it. On the other hand, who would she be friends with if everyone else was involved in an exclusive relationship?

22

When the final bell rang, Susie said, "Be right back, Mary."

Mary looked up from her assignment notebook. "I'll meet you in the hall."

Greg leaned across the aisle. "So what d'ya wanna do?" he asked her.

Mary's whole body tensed. "I'm going to Susie's," she told him. Judging by the girls' conversation at lunch, she expected him to give her an argument.

Shrugging, Greg got to his feet. "Okay," he said and turned to leave the room.

Mary relaxed. Greg was still Greg. He hadn't turned into some green-eyed monster. He had merely taken his role-playing too seriously. She'd have to talk to him about that.

She found Susie at her locker. Greg was there, too.

"What're you doing this afternoon, Greg?" Mary asked.

"Going to Susie's," he answered.

Mary shot Susie an inquiring look.

Susie smiled. "I didn't think you'd mind," she said.

She glowered at Greg. "No," she said. "I don't mind. Why should I mind?"

They walked three abreast toward Susie's house. Greg kept listing to the right toward Mary, who would then career into Susie.

Susie laughed. " 'Two's company, three's a crowd, four on the sidewalk not allowed,' " she chanted.

Finally, Mary said, "Greg, why don't you walk behind us or something."

Greg's mouth drooped sadly. She had hurt his feelings.

"The sidewalk's so narrow," she added to soften the blow.

"I know what," Susie piped up. "Put Greg in the middle."

Greg beamed. In his new position, he leaned left.

Mary finally stepped off the sidewalk and trudged along on the grass. It was a very long six blocks.

Things were no better at Susie's. Anywhere that Mary went, Greg was sure to go. He followed her to the sink for a drink of water, stood at her elbow in the candy room, and sat close beside her at the dining room table for a game of *Pictionary*.

"Don't sit so close," she told him. "You'll see my words."

"I won't look," he assured her.

When Susie's friend Nicky phoned, Mary made an excuse to leave. "But you can stay, Greg," she said.

"That's okay," Greg responded. "I'll walk you home."

Outside Susie's, Greg took Mary's hand.

She pulled it away. "You don't have to do that, Greg," she said. "No one's around. You can stop acting."

"A good actor lives his part," he said. "Onstage and off."

Mary made a face.

"You're too tense," he told her. "Try a little *t'ai chi*." He stopped walking, spread his feet, and bent his elbows shoulder height, arms dangling. "Chicken," he identified.

He looked so silly Mary couldn't help but laugh.

Greg phoned at seven-thirty. "So what's new?" he asked.

Mary laughed. "Nothing," she said. "How could anything be new? I just saw you two hours ago."

"So what should we talk about?" he asked.

"I don't know, Greg. What'd you want to talk about?"

"Beats me," he said.

Next morning, instead of waiting for her at the corner, Greg turned up at her house.

"Greg's waiting outside for you," her mother announced simply, but Mary heard her unspoken question: "What's going on?"

Sighing, Mary said, "I think he's practicing to be a bodyguard."

Outside, Greg said, "I've decided I'll pick you up here every day."

"You don't have to do that, Greg," Mary objected. "It's out of your way."

"I don't mind," he said.

Mary did mind. She didn't want him waiting outside her door. It would make her nervous. And what if he were late? Was she supposed to wait for him? That would make her more nervous. She liked the casual way they met now. But she didn't say so. She was afraid she'd hurt his feelings.

But the following week when he suggested they do their homework together every night after supper, she exploded.

"Grr-*egg*! This is getting ridiculous. We see each other so much now we don't even have anything to talk about anymore."

"You don't like being my girlfriend, is that what you're saying, Mags?" he asked.

"We're *supposed* to be pretending, Greg!" she reminded him.

He smiled sheepishly. "Can I help it if I'm so good at it?"

She stamped her feet in frustration.

"You're turning red," he said. "Relax. Breathe deeply. Concentrate."

There was absolutely no talking to him.

Or to anyone else.

23

No one seemed to be doing much talking. Jennifer was angry because Nina asked Matt if he was wearing a new jacket. Marisa was mad at Laurie for teasing Christopher about his height. Laurie was miffed with Richard because he kept spilling things. Tommy wasn't speaking to Amy because she went shopping with Jennifer without asking his permission. So many people were not speaking to so many other people, Mary couldn't keep track.

The class became so quiet that even Mrs. Anson was mystified. "What has happened to this class?" she asked. "Where's all that effervescence?"

Only Susie seemed her bubbly self.

There was much speculation about Susie's aloofness from the sixth-grade mania. Amy and some of the other girls decided she must have a boyfriend — probably someone from her old school.

At first, Mary was reluctant to accept that explanation, but she decided, finally, that the girls were probably right. Susie did have a boyfriend. That explained her indifference to the boys' attentions and her apparent knowledge of boy-girl relationships. It also explained why Susie was so happy all the time: Her boyfriend was far away where he couldn't bother her.

Mary decided, finally, she had to talk to Susie. Alone. But how was she going to get away from Greg long enough to do that?

She was trying to think of a solution to that problem one day when Mrs. Anson said, "We haven't discussed your projects in a long time."

No one knew what she was talking about.

Mrs. Anson laughed. "I guess it's been even longer than I thought!"

She gave them a few minutes to find their project lists and then she took an accounting. Several people were doing volcanoes. Mrs. Anson divided them into two groups. She put Nina and Marisa together to talk to plants. A few of the boys joined forces to test the life of batteries in warm and cold temperatures. A couple of others were working with Richard to determine whether bodies of different weights fell at the same rate. Although Greg was working alone, he was given permission to enlist the whole class' help with his *t'ai chi* experiments.

Finally, Mrs. Anson called on Mary.

"I still don't have an idea, Mrs. Anson," Mary said as she untucked her hair from behind her right ear.

Susie popped to her feet. "Mrs. Anson, could Mary and I work together?" she asked.

"What's your idea, Susie?" the teacher asked.

Mary cringed. She had a feeling that Susie didn't have an idea either. She untucked the hair from behind her left ear.

"I don't exactly have one," Susie said. "But if Mary and I could work together . . . " Her voice trailed off.

Mrs. Anson looked amused. "Well, I suppose two heads *are* better than one," she said.

"Not when there's nothing in either of them," Tommy mumbled.

But suddenly Mary did have an idea. Extrasensory Perception! It had been right there under her nose all along! Susie had been hinting at it. "We do have an idea," she said. "We just don't want to talk about it yet."

She smiled at Susie, who was staring at her with wide-eyed surprise.

During recess, Mrs. Anson conferred with the two girls privately and gave them approval.

"Maybe we could get together after school," Mary said to Susie. This was just the solution she'd been looking for: a reason to be with Susie without Greg tagging along.

"Nicky's coming over," Susie said. Her blue eyes gleamed happily.

Mary couldn't hide her disappointment.

"Why don't you come to my house anyway?" Susie suggested.

Mary hesitated. How could they work on the project or talk about events in the sixth grade with some strange girl hanging around? On the other hand, Nicky lived far away. Maybe she'd leave early. "If you're sure it's okay."

Susie beamed. "Nicky'd love to meet you."

Mary didn't have the chance to talk to Greg then. And when Mrs. Anson asked him to stay after school along with another boy, to discuss their projects in more detail, Mary decided not to tell him where she was going. If she did, he would probably give her an argument or find some excuse to tag along.

When the bell rang, he said, "Wait for me outside, Mary."

"I have to get home," she told him. "I'll talk to you later."

Mary skipped outside to meet Susie.

As they crossed the street, Mary said, "Our

project'll be great! I'm sure glad you thought of it."

Susie looked surprised. "I didn't think of it, Mary. You did."

"But you kept talking about how with my feelings and everything I should come up with a project," Mary said.

"I didn't think of using your psychic feelings *as* the project," Susie said. "I just thought you'd have a feeling about what your project should be."

"But you brought the cards and everything."

"They're my brother's. He did a term paper on ESP and I thought you'd like to have them is all."

"You gave Greg his idea," Mary said.

Susie laughed. "Me? No, I didn't. He kept saying *t'ai chi* exercises were relaxing, and I thought they'd be good to do while he was doing his project — you know, to relax him and help him think."

Mary had never met anyone so reluctant to take credit. It was a refreshing quality. "Well, anyway," she said, "we have a project. That's the important thing. And it'll be fun working on it." She glanced back over her shoulder half expecting to see Greg galloping toward them. She was relieved to find the coast clear. She returned her attention to Susie. "Are you sure she won't mind?"

"Who?"

"Nicky," Mary said.

Susie laughed. "Nicky's a *he* — not a *she*."

After a pause, Mary said, "Nicky's a . . . *boy*?!" Letting the full significance sink in, Mary felt as though she had just received the last piece in a puzzle. Susie did indeed, have a boyfriend! Nicky! Mary should have known!

"What's he look like?" Mary asked.

Susie shrugged. "Tall and sorta blond."

"Is he good-looking?"

"I guess. I never thought much about *that*."

Mary slipped her arm through Susie's. "I can't wait to meet him," she said.

As they rounded the corner to Oleander Street, Susie said, "There he is now!"

Ahead, a tall, thin young man was unfolding himself from the driver's side of a beat-up sports car.

Susie darted ahead. "Nicky!" she called.

Watching for Nicky to emerge from the passenger side, Mary picked up her pace.

The driver waved and smiled.

Susie flew into his arms. "Nicky! Nicky!" she said.

The boy responded with a laughing embrace.

Mary stopped cold. Her mouth dropped open. This was Nicky? He had to be at least *sixteen*!

The boy stood back. "How do you like my new car, Suz?" he asked proudly.

Susie laughed. "You call that *new*?"

"It's new to me," he joked.

Susie poked his arm. "Very funny!" she said.

They were so easy with one another. It reminded Mary of her and Greg — the way they used to be.

Smiling broadly, Susie turned to her. "Mary," she said, "this is Nicky."

Mary stepped forward.

Nicky beamed at her. "So this is the famous Mary. I'm really glad to meet you. Susie talks about you all the time."

Mary shifted from one foot to the other. She couldn't think of anything to say.

"Mary thought you were a girl," Susie told him.

Mary wanted to drop through the pavement.

Nicky laughed. "Well, if you'd call me Nick like everybody else, Suz, people wouldn't make that mistake."

Susie made a face. "I like *Nicky* better." She indicated the car. "Can we have a ride?"

Just then, an upstairs window opened and Susie's brother, Paul, leaned out. "Yo, Nick!" he called. "Come on up."

Nicky loped toward the house.

157

"What about our ride?" Susie asked him.

"Later," Nicky answered.

Watching after him, Susie said, "Isn't he nice?"

"Real nice," Mary agreed. "But isn't he . . . kinda old?"

Susie looked puzzled. "Old? For what?"

"To be your . . . boyfriend?"

Susie laughed. "Oh, Mary," she said, "Nicky's not my boyfriend! He's my *friend*."

24

"**N**icky's your *friend*?" Mary repeated.

"Actually, he was Paul's friend first," Susie explained. "They were in the same class, but he helped me with math sometimes, and we got to be friends, too."

Mary began to giggle. "I thought he was your *boyfriend*!"

Susie made a face. "I wouldn't want him for a boyfriend. I wouldn't want anyone for a boy-friend," she said. "Friends are more fun."

"For sure!" Mary agreed. Friendship was definitely better than romance — at least for now. She knew that, and yet she had let herself get trapped into playing the game while Susie had remained free. "You are so *smart*, Susie," she said. "You are *really* smart." Then, standing right there on the curb, she told Susie everything.

Susie listened with interest, interjecting an occasional, "Uh-huh," or "Really?" or "That's awful!"

"We were supposed to be pretending," Mary concluded, "only now I think Greg might not be pretending anymore and he's no fun to be with — neither am I! I keep hurting his feelings and everytime I say anything, he tells me to breathe deeply and do Repulse Monkey or stand like a chicken or something, and I don't know what to do."

"Just tell him you want to go back to being friends," Susie advised.

Mary thought about that. It seemed to make perfect sense. And so simple. There must be a catch somewhere. She thought of one, "But how can I tell him? It'll hurt his feelings."

"Just say it straight out," Susie told her. "You're probably hurting his feelings all the time, because you're acting different. If you just go back to being yourself . . . ." She shrugged.

Susie had a point. Mary *was* a different person around Greg these days. Where before she had been open and accepting, she had closed down and become critical. She had even lied to him today! Being her honest self might work with Greg. It was certainly worth a try. But what would the rest of the class think? If she and Greg did go back to being friends, what would they think? "What about everybody else?" she asked.

Susie waved that away. "They'll never notice. They've got their own problems."

Mary laughed. "For sure!" Straightening with determination, she added, "I should go over to Greg's right this minute." The project could wait. At the moment, this was far more important. "Maybe you could meet us later, Susie."

Susie nodded. "After Nicky and Paul leave." She smiled warmly. "Go for it, Mary!"

Greg was on his garage roof.

"Come down," Mary directed. "We have to talk."

Greg glared down at her. "You weren't home," he said accusingly.

"I was at Susie's."

"I know. Your mother told me."

"It was the only way I could get away from you, Greg," she explained. "If I told you I was going to Susie's . . . " She couldn't talk to him like this; the whole neighborhood would hear her. "Come down, Greg. I have to talk to you."

He squinted down at her. After a long pause, he said, "What about?"

He was so infuriating.

"I don't want to be your girlfriend anymore — pretend or not — that's what about!" She pivoted sharply and marched up his drive.

She heard a thud behind her and suddenly he was at her side.

"Why not?"

Coming to a dead halt, she whirled to face him. "Because you're no fun anymore, that's why!" she shouted.

He guffawed. "And you are?" He leaned in so close their noses touched. "You don't want to be my girlfriend? That's just great, because I don't want to be your boyfriend either!"

Her hands flew to her hips. "Nothing could make me happier, Greg Hopkins!"

"So we're both happy!"

He was so close her eyes crossed. "Yes!"

He backed off. "Then why are we shouting?"

She couldn't help it. She laughed. And then he did, too!

"Oh, Greg," she said as soon as she had control of herself again, "I'm so glad you're not mad at me."

"I thought it'd be a good idea, you and me . . . " He shrugged.

"You're just too good an actor, Greg. That's all. You even convinced yourself!"

"And the more I believed I really *liked* you," he said, "the less I liked you."

She knew exactly what he meant.

"And besides, romance," he wiggled his eyebrows like Groucho Marx, "takes up too much time. Do you realize I even missed two *t'ai chi* classes to spend time with you?"

"That's not my fault, Greg," she said. "I didn't ask you to spend all that time with me. I didn't *want* you to do that."

His eyes twinkled. "Do you think that made it any easier?"

Mary gave him a swat. "Oh, you!" she said.

As they ambled out of the drive, he said, "I'm sure glad that's over!"

Mary cocked her head to look at him. "It was pretty awful," she said. But she felt she had learned from the experience. She'd never again try to play a role she wasn't ready for. And she'd always be honest with friends no matter what.

Greg broke into her thoughts with a poke.

She followed his gaze. They were approaching Mrs. Popek's wall.

He raised an eyebrow. "What d'ya think?"

Laughing, she began to race him to the rock wall.

Though he could easily outrun her, he hung

back. "You're really gonna do it, huh, Mary?" he said as she climbed atop the wall.

Standing triumphantly on top, her arms outspread, she said, "I *am* doing it!"

He clambered up beside her, and, with Mary as leader, they made their way along the wall.

"You kids get down from there!" Mrs. Popek hollered.

Together they jumped back down and ran away, laughing.

They were still laughing when they got to Sweet 'n' Ice.

Some of their classmates waved to them from a table in the corner. They all looked glum.

"What'll you have?" Greg asked Mary.

Just as she always did, Mary studied the menu on the wall behind the counter.

"As if I didn't know," Greg added under his breath.

"I think I'll have a doubleheader," Mary said. "One blueberry cheesecake and one peanut butter."

Greg reeled back. Then, recovering, he placed his hands on his stomach and doubled over. "Order me a doctor," he joked.

Nina stared at them enviously. "They always

have so much fun together," she said. "Why do they always have so much fun?"

Mary overheard her. Smiling at Greg, she explained, "We're friends. Friends always have fun together."

Greg returned her smile. *"That's* what friends are for," he said.

APPLE® PAPERBACKS

Pick an Apple and Polish Off Some Great Reading!

NEW APPLE TITLES

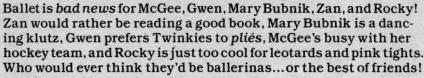

Pack your bags for fun and adventure with

SLEEPOVER FRIENDS™
by Susan Saunders